Millionaire Dreams

Written By
Alechy Sumter

Dedication

-From Now Until Forever It'll Always Be About B.K.B and A.L.B

Acknowledgments

This one is all for my cousins. Especially the ones who slept on the floor with me at Grandma Channey house. I love ya'll crazy asses! Robert, Rashard(Squid), Jamaze(Fif Trump) Tiffany, Tearia, Taneisha(Czai), Tanarda(Chante), Tashara(Do) Brandon(Mr.B), Antonio(Puff), Precious(Pretty P), Ambrea, Ya'll are always one phone call away!!

PROLOGUE

Major counted the money for the second time before sliding the stacks across the table to his connect. "Yeah, my nigga, that's eleven-five on the dot."

"And, this girl, is right at five hundred grams," Fresh confirmed for his partner in crime.

"Nigga, you know my work is always accurate. I don't even know why y'all weighed the package behind me," Rico said, as he rolled the White Rhino weed in a mini Swisher Sweets cigarillo.

"Nigga, the same reason you had me recount my money!" Major replied. "Nigga, you need to leave me that other five hundred grams of coke you got wit you."

"You know I would, but I'm bout to tax a nigga right quick in Highland Forest," Rico replied sincerely, as he lit his blunt and headed towards the door to leave. "Y'all get back at me. I'm out."

Major and Fresh escorted him outside. They wanted to check the surroundings and make sure he reached his whip safely before they hit the kitchen to water whip crack cookies. The dope boys were hungry and ready to eat. The re-up always kept them lined up in droves. Rico got into the passenger side of his silver Dodge Ram pick-up, and the high yellow, red headed female he had driving backed up and pulled out of the parking lot. As they were leaving, a city police car was pulling in, but for some reason, the police busted a U-turn and threw the blue lights on behind Rico's truck.

"Damn!" Major said as he watched the encounter take place from his position in Selah's hallway. I know they gon' search the truck. Rico just sparked fire to the ass end of the blunt. "Shit!" Major exclaimed shaking his head while thinking of the inevitable.

"A trip to the county seems to be in Rico's near future," he added.

"Not if I have something to do with it. Fuck that shit!" Fresh said as he walked by a near dumpster and grabbed a solid pipe. "I ain't 'bout to let bruh go to jail. Not tonight. Not on my watch."

Major gave Fresh a curious look. "Boy, what the fuck you about to do?" Major inquired with a serious expression decorating his face.

Puffing his Newport and clutching the pipe with his other hand he responded, "grown man shit. I ain't lettin' Rico get caught with that fuckin' half-brick. Fuck nah!" Fresh thumped his cigarette and trotted to the side of the 15 building to get closer to the street without being obvious.

As the officer stepped from the police cruiser, Fresh observed that he was young and black. *Damn I wish he was white, but it is what it's about to be.* Fresh's heart beat rapidly within his chest cavity, palms sweating, and his thoughts were traveling at lighting speeds. If it were Major in this situation, the police would've probably gotten shot because he loved Major that much. Fresh was a team player and knew his position, so handling this matter was only a part of his role in the streets. He quietly eased behind the police officer as he slowly approached Rico's truck. Before the officer could pass the gas cap, Fresh was about four feet behind him.

The officer must've sensed Fresh's presence because he slightly turned around, only catching a quick glimpse of his attacker's face before having the thick, steel pipe slammed across his right eye, instantly splitting his temple wide open, knocking him unconscious. "Bitch ass muthafucka." He grunted before kicking him in the ribs for good measure.

Fresh walked to the passenger side of Rico's truck, "ride out, my nigga! I apologize to yo' girl for having to witness g-shit, but I couldn't let you go down with all that work you riding with."

"Goddamn, you was right on time! Preciate that, bruh, for real. I'll get with you later. You know I'ma look out for you," Rico divulged before giving the female the ok to pull off.

Fresh walked over to the officer, kicked him a few more times, and removed the Glock 40 from his hip, then he trotted back across the street and camouflaged himself with the people he grew up with in the hood.

Someone eventually called the paramedics to come help the officer. Within minutes the area was swarmed with police. Bands of officers fitted in black full riot gear descended upon the hood resembling black ants as they separated going from door to door asking questions. One of their own had been severely injured and various forms of law enforcement wanted answers. They were casing the apartments with military grade rifles in hand. They were ready for war, fully trained for action. They never found the person responsible because no one was brave enough to turn state on Fresh. He was volatile and quick to bust his gun. Nobody wanted the barrel of his weapon pointed at their top piece.

For weeks, the hood was on fire. No illicit drug transactions could take place without interference from the law. Other hustlers were upset that they couldn't sell their drugs without being harassed or locked up, but they knew how shit went in the hood. Niggas had to find another location to hustle until it cooled down or continue to take chances because the city police had officers posted in every parking lot from sunup to sundown.

The city narcotics even stopped by on a daily basis, searching whoever they saw, but no matter how severe the harassment, no one uttered a word.

Fresh and Major chilled out for a while with the hustling. Like possums, they only came out at night, riding around the city robbing other dope boys.

Rico had met up with Fresh and gave him five grand for preventing him a big loss (a trip to jail and hefty lawyer fees). He knew if he didn't play fair, he would become prey. He would certainly make Fresh's list of persons to jack if he hadn't come correct on some paper.

Officer Steeples laid up in Richland Memorial Hospital for a few weeks with a fractured skull, which needed a minor operation. Staples resembling a zipper crowned his head and he had several broken ribs. During his stay in the hospital, all he could think about was getting revenge. He couldn't get the vision of the guy's face out of his mind and promised himself to make him suffer.

Pussy ass dope boys think they can fuck with me. I'm the law! I'ma make all they asses pay. All of them gon' bow at my feet, he promised himself. Not being home with his wife and child did something to his spirit. The fact that he had allowed a street nigga to get the drop on him caused him to feel like less than a man. Brian laid up in the hospital for weeks recovering from his injuries. When they gave him his discharge papers, he was a ruined deputy. One out for blood and revenge...

You Lose...

Blade sighed deeply as a combination of stress and fatigue weighed him down. Working at the painting company had physically worn him out. Yet, mentally he pondered over where his next high would come from. He scratched at his arms as withdrawal symptoms crept into his mind. If he didn't get a hit soon, he'd be sicker than a cancer patient. The monkey on his back threatened to become an untamed gorilla if he didn't get high with a quickness. He didn't get paid until Friday, and it was just Tuesday. Blade wanted to get high really badly but had no idea where he was going to come up with the money. *Somebody will front me something on the face til I get paid*, he surmised.

When he walked into his friend Calvin's apartment in the Willow Run apartment complex where he and his girlfriend Feebi lived, the smell of rocks being smoked tickled his nostrils. He picked up his pace, following the crack scent down the hallway. When he pushed open the room door, his eyes twinkled as he watched Feebi pushing her stem with a tv antenna.

"Damn, baby, you ain't save none for me?" Blade asked defeated as Feebi's eyes rolled into the back of her head. Slob fell from the corner of her mouth as the potent drug invaded her lungs. Feebi ignored him in her euphoric state.

"Feebi!" he exclaimed, kicking at her thigh with his booted foot to rouse her.
After a long day of hard work, he at least expected to be greeted with a cheerful "hello", but Feebi paid his ass no attention. No hug, no kiss, no "hey, baby", just a straight cold stare.

"What the fuck ,Blade, damn!" she fussed, snapping out of her stupor.

"You really know how to ruin a bitch's high, shit! All I had was a little piece of rock. That shit wasn't enough to share, barely got me right. Why don't you take my EBT card and see if you can get one of them boys to give you some'n for the two hundred I have on there," Feebi offered.

Right on time. Blade thought. "Alright, where it's at?" Feebi pulled the EBT card from her bra. Soon as he saw the fruit on the small piece of plastic, Blade hastily snatched the card from Feebi's hand and headed out the door. "Snatch something from me again, you broke muthafucka. You ain't in that much of a rush to get high that damn bad, bitch!"

Blade ignored Feebi's rant as he proceeded out the door. She was always hostile and talking shit when she was full of crack, but Blade loved her crazy, junkie ass.

Feebi walked out of the room she'd been in and knocked on Cal's bedroom door before entering. When she walked in, she saw him putting fire to his stem. "Let me hit that. When Blade come back with our shit, we'll share with you."

Cal held the stem out for her to take. "Here."

Feebi rocked back and forth while hitting the pipe knowing that she was dead ass wrong for giving Blade an empty EBT card, but she needed some crack, fuck how she got it. She just hoped he didn't go to Major with it. She and Cal sat at on the foot of his bed pushing their empty stems, while hoping Blade was successful on his mission.

Willow Run Projects was live with dope boys and money hungry, blunt smoking, pill popping slut buckets posted everywhere, but Blade went to the group of dope boys who always posted on the brick wall behind building 16. They had the best dope. As he walked past the 14 building, dope boys hollered at him to come cop from them because they knew he always spent money. But Blade chucked them the deuces and kept stepping. A functioning addict, Blade got up every day for work to have money to nurse his habit and provide for Feebi and their daughter as best he could.

"Fuck you too, mufucka," Mook yelled at his back. He was the neighborhood asshole. No one really fucked with him like that, only tolerated his ass. "I know that's right, and it's all good. When them niggas won't serve you with that short change, remember that."

"Nah Mook, it ain't like that, I'm just tryna get off this EBT card," Blade replied as he kept walking, holding the SNAP card in the air.

"Yeah, whatever. Like I said, you gon' need me when you and yo' bitch broke."

As Blade got by the 15 building, he spotted who he was looking for sitting on the wall smoking a cigarette.

"What's up, fellas?"

"What up, Blade?" Major, Fresh, and Von replied in unison.

"Aye, Major, I got this EBT with $200 on it. Let me get some'n nice for it. I'm jonesing like a mutha right now."

"Let me see it," Major said as he reached for the card. He looked at the name, then shook his head. "Hell no. I ain't serving you or Feebi," he spat.

He couldn't believe that Feebi was trying to play him like that. He hopped down from the brick wall he was sitting on and threw the card in Blade's face.

Major had been in a foul mood all day. After running the streets, paying pills, and taking care of personal business, he had come back to the hood and discovered somebody had crept two ounces of crack from him.

"Man, what the fuck you threw the shit at me like that for? I ain't never disrespect you, Major," Blade stated in his defense.

"Nigga, Feebi already sold me this insufficient shit, but she got my dope and turned the card off on some slick shit. Had my people in the grocery store with a buggy full of shit, and the card kept declining. Now you tryna do the shit again," Major surmised with a snarl.

"Man, I don't know nuttin' bout that shit! I just got off of work. Let me see what the hell is going on. I wouldn't play no games with you about no money," Fresh chuckled. "Nigga, you's a junkie. You'll do anything to smoke some dope. Fuck out of here with that bullshit." He reminded with a wave of his hand.

"Nah, fuck that shit, nigga! You already know what that bitch up to! Just tell me where she at, and I'll go holla at her myself.".

"Man, I don't know where she at. Just let me get this shit straight," Blade said, noticing the look Major had on his face.

Major punched Blade in his face with a sneak blow, but Blade wasn't scared. He took the lick and posted up in a fighting stance. Blade swung back, but Major, Fresh, and Von jumped on him. When Blade was able to stand on his feet, they assumed he would walk off, but Blade pulled a knife from his pocket. Ready to poke the hell out of one of them with it.

Selah, Von's sister, saw Blade with the knife and crept up behind him with a brick in the palm of her small hand. *Whap*! She struck Blade in the back of his head with all the power she possessed. Dazed, Blade fell to his knees and dropped the knife. Von and Fresh charged Blade at full force, scooping him by the legs before slamming him to the ground. It felt like a wrecking ball crashing into his fragile body. Once he collided with the pavement, Von joined in and the two commenced to beating him while he was on the ground, but Major had other intentions. He picked up the knife from the ground. He was the nice guy. Always looking out for people, yet always got shitted on in the end. He refused to be played like a game of tag. Fuck that. This time he wouldn't be "it". He'd grown tired of people trying to play him for a sucker in this petty ass dope game. He ran up on Blade after pushing the homies out of his path.

"Oh, you pulling knives on niggas now, Blade?" Major snarled with his upper lip curled. He was baffled by the gall of this smoker. Major raised the knife high above his head, slashing it through the air with so much force, people standing nearby could hear the swoosh. He plunged the knife into Blade's back leaving the sharp object lodged inside him.

Blade felt stinging combined with pressure in his back, but he didn't realize he'd been stabbed until he felt wetness behind him and pulled the knife out. Seeing his blood on the blade caused him to become faint. For the past few months, he'd been carrying that knife and never thought he'd actually be stabbed with his own weapon.

"Mufucka! You ain't have to stab me, but don't worry, I'ma get back at y'all," Blade threatened as he trotted off heading back to Calvin's house to call an ambulance. He knew that he required medical attention because the entire knife, minus the handle, had been left in his back.

Blade wanted to stab Major back, but with Von pointing his gun at him, there was nothing he could've done. Walking as if he had a hump in his back, Blade walked through the apartments to return back to Calvin's.

Mook saw Blade struggling to carry himself on his own two feet and clowned him.
"Yeah, mufucka, you done went to the wall and got ya ass beat. I told you to holla at us, but nah. Now, look at you. That's what yo' ass get," Mook teased, as he noticed the way Blade was walking with his t-shirt bloody.

"Fuck you," Blade replied as he kept walking, hoping he didn't pass out. He made a mental note to fuck Mook up the first chance he got.

Blade knocked on Calvin's door to his apartment in Helendale, which was across the road from Willow Run. When Calvin opened the door, Blade asked Cal for his sawed off shotgun, which he had given the name "Baby".

"Nigga is you crazy?! Don't nobody finger Baby but me."

"Man let me get Baby, Cal, straight up. This shit serious."

"Hell nah, nigga! Why, what's up?" Cal asked.

Blade grimaced in pain as he pulled his shirt over his head showing Cal his injury.

"Them young niggas jumped on me, and Major had the nerve to stab me in my damn back. I'ma kill those niggas!"

"Man, I ain't givin' you my gun. Fuck what you talkin' bout."

"Fuck it then, just call me an ambulance."

"Ain't nobody told you to go up there fucking with those people. I don't want them mufuckas comin' to my house man. I got too much goin' on here already. I can't get put out behind you and Feebi bullshit," Cal informed with finality. He was really scared to get involved in any way because he knew how crazy those young boys could get.

"Nigga, if you don't call me some damn help, I'ma just bleed out and die right here in yo' fuckin' livin' room. See if you'll like white chalk decorating your floor, and where is that no good bitch at anyway. She coulda told me that she had already fucked over the boy Major, but it's cool. I'ma skin her ass when I catch her. Dirty bitch knew that's who I was gon' go to. Fuck her and Major."

Calvin finally decided to call an ambulance. He thought about Blade dying in his apartment and didn't want his death on his hands.

Nickel Slick...

"Feebi, why don't you run to Flying J's and make a quick hundred, so we can get high, instead of sitting here with me pushing these empty ass stems? Hell, if I had a pussy and a body like yours, I would never be broke," Cal said, hoping to convince her to go tricking.

"Nigga, yo' half dead ass can't pimp me. If I go sell my pussy, I ain't sharing that shit with you. Besides, I ain't goin' trickin' unless Blade with me, but don't worry 'bout how I get mine, just know I gets it."

"Well, bitch, you can't keep layin' up in here for free. That lil' blast you gave me ain't did shit. Garbage ass dope ain't even make my heart beat fast. You shoulda took Blade with you to the truck stop instead of sendin' that man on a suicide mission. You gon' be the death of that man," Cal warned shaking his head. He knew she had done the fuck shit because he was the one that called the EBT card in missing.

"That's his stupidity, not mine," she said while peeping out of the living room window to see what was taking Blade so long, and to her surprise, he was limping up the sidewalk, bleeding.

"Damn" she said to herself. Then, without saying a word to Cal, Feebi quietly eased out of the back door.

Feebi stood to the side of the building listening to what Blade had to say when he entered the apartment. She heard the whole story and, of course, didn't feel a bit of shame or remorse for the pain and embarrassment she caused.

"Fuck it, that's just how life is. It's fucked up sometimes." She justified before heading to the Flying J's truck stop to get her trick on. *"What the fuck am I moping about? I might as well go and treat myself to some dick and a few dollars in the process while Blade getting patched up at the hospital. No need in crying over spilled milk. The damage has been done.* She told herself as she walked down Fairfield Road.

As Feebi walked past the gas pumps, she noticed one of the truckers flick his headlights at her. She went to the red rig and climbed into the passenger side.

"What's up, Chocolate? What's it gon' cost you to make a country boy's knees buckle?" The fat, Caucasian trucker held a strong resemble to Guy Fieri. The chubby man from the Food Network, stiff hair and all.

"Thirty for a BJ and fifty to fuck," she replied.

"And what about a combination of both?" he questioned with a smile, allowing his eyes to roam all over her frame.

Feebi licked her lips. "Give me seventy and let's make it happen."

The trucker peeled seventy dollars from his wallet, then unfastened his belt and unbuttoned his dirty wrangler jeans while pulling them down to his knees.

Feebi pulled a condom from her bra. She bit the foil off using her mouth to slide the condom onto his manhood. With a little assistance from her right hand, she tugged at his pink meat to get him rocked up.

Feebi devoured his small member. Swallowing his meat whole. "Lord, have mercy. Yes, honey. Suck it for me. Suck it all," he encouraged, pumping into her mouth. After three minutes of oral sex, the trucker prematurely ejaculated into the condom. Feebi felt his body jerk and quiver. That's when she pushed herself up to exit the truck, but he was dissatisfied.

"Hold on where you goin', baby? You were paid for a little of both. You still owe me some pussy."

Feebi looked at the trucker with a sour face. "You got yo' nut. I'm outta here," she said reaching for the door handle to let herself out, but she was stopped by the firm grip he had on her wrist.

"If you not gonna uphold your end of the bargain, give me some of my money back. You said thirty for some head, so now you owe me forty dollars."

"Alright, damn! Let me get another condom from my purse," she relented.

Feebi went into her purse, but instead of pulling out another condom, she came out with a box cutter and went to slicing and dicing the trucker. She was carving him up like slicing deli meat. He fought her, but she was too swift with the blade. The trucker hit the horn by accident numerous times trying to defend himself. He desperately wanted to get away from the psychotic woman with the good blow job and box cutter. He fought tirelessly and eventually he was able to get the door opened, but he fell to the ground as he tried to escape the crazed woman. He'd forgotten that he didn't have his pants pulled up. The tussling with Feebi had caused them to rest around his ankles.

A Richland County patrol car pulled into front of the truck after hearing the horn honking repeatedly. He witnessed the trucker falling out of the rig and immediately drew his weapon.

"Hands above your head! Do not move!" The officer ordered the trucker.

"Please, officer, that woman is trying to kill me!" he cried using his white privilege while pointing at his rig.

Feebi frantically looked all around her. *I ain't going to jail, not today.*

Feebi decided to get out and make a run for it, but she was moving so quickly, she had completely forgotten about how far the rig was from the pavement, that she fell out of the truck also. The officer ran to her and noticed that she was covered in blood. The boxcutter was still in Feebi's grip. When the sun bounced off the metal tip, he pulled his gun, "ma'am, drop the blade and lay on the ground."

Feebi dropped the blade like he asked, but she wasn't getting on the ground like he demanded her to. It was damn near a hundred degrees outside; she wasn't laying on that hot ass pavement. Instead, she decided to take her chances by running. She didn't anticipate things transpiring the way they had. Things had gotten out of control too quickly. She didn't intend for this to happen.

But at the same time, Feebi couldn't fathom waking up in county. It was too hot to be sitting in anyone's jail. Not to mention the withdrawals her body would endure if she couldn't post bail. All these thoughts raced through her mind as she took off sprinting in the opposite direction. *I can't go to jail. Not today.*

All she had on her mind was the next blast of crack rock. As Feebi ran, heading for the intersection towards the Texaco gas station, car horns blared as she was nearly struck by oncoming traffic. Feebi's chest was on fire as she ran for dear life. *If I reach North 21 Terrace, I can shake his ass.* She concluded hyping herself up.

Feebi glanced over her shoulder and noticed the officer was gaining on her. She picked up speed, but her efforts were futile. The officer was too fast for her trot. Feebi felt like she was running a hundred miles per hour, but she was running at crackhead speed. The police officer had the speed and agility of a football athlete compared to her pace. "Stop! Don't make me tase you. Stop, right now!" the officer yelled at her back as he shortened the distance between them.

The officer lunged at Feebi's back, tackling her to the ground as if he were preventing her from scoring the winning touchdown. "Get off me, bitch! Fuck you, muthafucka!" she cursed nastily as the officer tried securing her thin wrist in cuffs. She bit, kicked and even tried kneeing him in the nuts, but her efforts were blocked. Feebi fought relentlessly to no avail.

She was acting a damn fool. The officer had no choice but to use brute force in restraining her. On her side, screaming obscenities, she hawked spit into the officer's face. The thick glob clung to his skin, infuriating him.

"You junkie bitch!" He grunted before placing his knee into her back. "Agghh, you hurting me!" she hollered as he twisted her arms like a pretzel to handcuff her.

The officer called for backup while half walking, half dragging Feebi back towards his patrol car. She continued to buck like a bull, and he continued snatching her itty bitty ass back up.

As they approached, the officer noticed the trucker on the ground with blood covering his face. His pants when still down and around his ankles.

Feebi smirked and showed no remorse for the carnage she had done. The trucker's face and arms were covered in deep lacerations from the boxcutter. The officer radioed dispatch. "I'll also need an ambulance. Victim bleeding about the arms and face at the Flying J gas station on Fairfield Road," the officer finished breathlessly. Tussling with Feebi had worn him out.

Once he finished with dispatch, he read Feebi her rights. "Ma'am you have the right to remain silent-"

"Nigga fuck you. I know my muthafuckin rights, bitch!" Feebi interjected before he could Mirandize her.

He opened the door to the patrol car, slinging Feebi into the backseat like discarded trash. Feebi leaned back attempting to kick out the windows of the squad car. The car rocked sideways as she behaved like a caged gorilla.

Feebi was charged with prostitution, aggravated assault, resisting arrest, and assault to an officer. Once the paramedics patched the trucker up, he was also booked for indecent exposure and solicitation.

Motivation...

Major and Selah laid up in her queen sized bed blowing clouds of Purple Thrax while watching Baller Blockin'. He was heavily inspired by the way Baby and Slim had Cash Money Millionaires on the map, eating in a major way. He knew if they could come out of the trenches and end up on top, so could he.

"Selah, you see how them niggas eatin'? That's the level I'm tryna get on, not out here stuck in the projects, stabbing cluckaz and shit. I wanna be a millionaire but still be able to hang in the hood by choice, not by force, feel me?"

"Yeah, I hear you, boo, but that's tv, and niggas ain't got all that work in real life," Selah responded.

"See, babe, that's where you wrong. Them niggas are the Cash Money Millionaires and you best believe that them boys were caked up and had batter before they got in the music game. But, what I'm speakin' on, is how they doin' movies now. Yeah, they've had a lot of strife within the clique, but look at the status they were able to garner. The respect and recognition they get from the streets. There's money to be made and I'm gonna stack mine in layers, just mark my word. It's his motivation, ambition, and drive that got me so influenced. We gotta stop thinking small and start thinking like a big timer, straight up. I'll never get comfortable having the minimum. I'm always focused on more and elevation. For real."

"I hear you. Whatever you down for, I'm with you one hundred," she said as she snuggled closer under Major's arm, loving his thought process and how he never hated on the next man.

As Major sat back blowing O's in the air, his thoughts were on elevating his status in the streets. He had grown tired of being a block boy and going half on petty ass quarter keys. Those nickels and dimes paid the bills, but he wanted all white bricks. Major saw himself as a boss and wanted to live up to his name.

At twenty years old, Major had been in the game since he was fourteen but had never touched a kilo, let alone seen one with his own two eyes. Only what he saw in movies and heard about glamorized in rap lyrics. As far as he was concerned, hood niggas with kilos was an urban legend. Until he touched his own, a brick was nothing but a figment of his imagination.

"Hold up, baby. I gotta pee right quick," Selah informed. Major moved his arm from around her slim waist and watched her phat ass jiggle as she walked out of the room.

Major sat up in bed glancing at his reflection in the mirror positioned beside the bed. "Major, you a boss. Everything you want, you have the ambition and drive to make it happen. Do what you gotta do to level the fuck up!" he encouraged himself. Daily he spoke BAWSE affirmations over his life.

He heard Selah's steps coming down the hallway.

She stretched in the doorway, watching Major watch her. "So, what we doing today, baby."

"Ion't know what you doing, but I'm about to pull outta this pussy and paper chase. You gonna have to find something to do with your time because I'm about to get on some other shit. Cop and re-up, that's what I'm doing today," Major filled her in. He couldn't level up if he was digging in her guts all day.

"I understand baby. I still have a few pieces leftover. I'll shake those off today. Probably go do female shit. Ti'ed of being in the hood all day."

"I feel ya', Selah. I gotta goal to reach. Watch my smoke, I'm about to have shit sewed the fuck up round here!" Major boasted, believing in himself. A better life was his for the taking.

Their conversation was interrupted by someone knocking on the bedroom door.
Major grabbed his .357 Smith & Wesson from the nightstand.

"What?" Selah answered.

"Sis, tell Major the nigga Mook wanna holla at' em right quick," Selah's younger brother Von responded from the hallway.

"I hope he ain't let that fake ass nigga in the apartment," Major said as he slipped on his Coogi sweat pants and tucked his gun in the waistband and hid two ounces of crack under his nuts.

He walked into the living room to see Mook and Big Ram standing by the door.

"What's up, y'all?" Major said.

"We wanna grab ah oz from you, bruh," Mook said. "It's shakin' out there."

"Aight." Major reached into his pants, retrieving the two ounces he had just concealed under his nuts and handed Mook one of the circles from the sandwich bag.

Mook handed Major five hundred dollars, "shid, you might as well let me get the other one on the face, and I'll have yo bread for you early in the mornin' because I ain't goin' to sleep tonight."

"Alright"

"I got you, Major! Thanks, bruh," Mook said and left out the door.

Tsk. Von kissed his teeth. "Bruh, you shouldn't have gave that nigga shit."

"Why? It ain't like you out there tryna get ahead of the game. Can't loathe a nigga cause he wanna eat good. You need to be tryna get yo belly full. Steada half assin' out here. Mook is a hustla and I'ma fuck with 'em as long as he play fair. I could care less about what he got going on in those streets. Ya' dig?"

Von looked at his feet as Major spoke. "I feel you, but I'ma step my shit up, you watch."

Major shrugged his shoulders. "Nigga, don't try to impress me. Do it because you want money. Watch how I elevate my hustle. I'm bout to take off. I'm bout to Young Dolla on y'all niggas. "Ambitions as a Millionaire" like a muthafucka, right under ya nose," Major said and headed back in the room with Selah.

Selah was a jazzy female. Willing to do whatever for the team. At least that's how she presented herself. She and her brother Von sold both crack and weed for Major. A brown bombshell with hazel eyes, Selah kinda puts you in the mind of a chocolate Stacy Dash, a hood beauty that niggas fawned over. Always about her grind, Major had her brother Von selling white for him while Selah sold the weed and sometimes crack, but she mainly just collected money people owed him. If it were up to him, Selah would have no parts of his illicit affairs, but she was the type of woman who felt the need to be a part of something whether the cause was good or bad. For now, he'd keep her on his team until she crossed that line. These hoes ain't loyal, and when given a little time, they always revealed their true intent.

Eat, Don't Compete...

Mook, Big Ram, Fresh, Von, and Major all grew up together in the same hood. Mook and Big Ram were always closer because their mothers were best friends, and they lived right next door to one another. Being that Big Ram was always a big dude and his last name is Ramsey, he was given the alias from his Pop Warner football coach, and it stuck with him.

Big Ram was a damn good football player since he played in the peewee league and aspired to play pro in the NFL. After graduating high school, he received a full ride to attend Georgia Tech University. A knee injury and bad grades gave him a one way ticket right back to the hood. Mook welcomed his return with open arms.

Mook was a solo hustler selling weed before Ram came back, but when he got a lil' muscle on his side and an extra mouth to feed, he decided to step his game up and sell a lil' crack. Smokers were plentiful in their hood. Therefore, there was money to be made. He invested a few hundred of his weed profits into a crack pack from Major and bought a seven gram quarter of crack and quickly flipped it into an ounce. Mook was a hustler, but he loved to shine for women, so clothes, jewels, and cars got a lot of his money. Big Ram wasn't really a hustler. He was more so Mook's lap dog who Mook used as security, but Mook looked out for Ram like a true friend should.

Mook and Ram lived in building 3 at the top of the hood, but they posted up and hustled by building 14 where Ram's girlfriend Tonya lived with her mom who smoked crack; so there was no problem with them hanging in front of the building, in her apartment, or in her hallway. A so called "player", Mook didn't have a woman. He felt that having a girl was a sucker move. Women were play things. Objects to drop his dick in for pleasure and nothing more. His saying was "why have one, when you can fuck 'em all?" That's the motto he lived by.

Mook and Big Ram shared a family sized bag of Flaming Hot Cheetos while posted on the block making money. The smokers were out in droves tonight, and the knot full of money that laced their pockets was motivation to keep on pushing. Mook yawned and stretched as they watched various people milling about the projects.

"Man, I'm glad we got that work from Major. He got that good dope. Look at how all the cluckaz pulling up," Big Ram said.

"Yeah, and if we keep pulling all-nighters while he lay up with Selah, all the cluckaz gon' be looking to spend with us because we are always posted. Graveyard shift gon' put us on, mark my words," Mook responded.

A smoker approached the duo looking tattered and worn. Smelling like a combination of feet and ass, the odor coming from his body spoke before he could. "Let me get a big rock for $20." He requested offering rolled up quarters for his high. Mook took the two rolls of quarters from his hand. He peeled the paper from around them to ensure that quarters were in the wrappings and not Chuck E Cheese tokens. Smokers were clever and conniving when they wanted to get high. They pulled all kinds of silly stunts for the drug.

"What we told you 'bout coming through here with that damn slot machine money?" Mook joked.

The smoker shook his head and scratched at his face while waiting on Big Ram to serve him. The funk coming from his body more pronounced with each movement. "I just wanna get right man. Whether that shit jingle or fold it, spends the same."

Mook fanned the air with his hand. The smell coming from the smoker made his eyes water. "You need to wash yo' ass. Goddamn, you stank man. Know you smelt yo' self before walking up here."

The smoker said nothing in response to Mook's remarks. He wanted to get high. He'd wash his ass when he felt like it.

Big Ram chuckled. "Damn right. I don't care how you bring it. I don't give a fuck if he had rolled up pennies; I take those too. Fuck with me, change and all." Big Ram reached into his pants, retrieved a bag of rocks from under his scrotum, then handed the man something to make him feel good. The man scurried along. Dipping into the woods on the other side of the road.

"But, back to Major. If he keeps fronting us work on the face, we'll reach brick status in no time. I can't wait to touch thirty-six ounces."

"Yep, we just gotta keep handling our bitness like how we doing and playing fair. Long as we keep our name good, a nigga will fuck with us. We'll probably be buying more work than him. I know Von and Fresh ain't stackin'. Them niggas don't hang long enough, but we gon' post during the day and get what we can get, and mainly focus on the graveyard shift, and watch how fast we blow." Mook countered, worrying about the next niggas pockets. He hustled to stunt for bitches and floss on Instagram.

"You got that shit right, bruh, tired of hustling backwards. I don't even wanna compete. I just wanna eat. Period. Stack my bread and live good. That's all I'm on. The key is to win, not to look like you winning. Feel me?"

"All this nigga do is give me diseases, dishonesty, and dirty dick. I can't wait until I can leave his ass. I'm so tired of loving his toxic ass!"

Quies sat on her black leather couch in the living room with all the lights off while she watched the front door finally open. He eased into the apartment quietly. "Look at his slick ass, tryna creep in at four o'clock in the fuckin' morning," Quies mumbled to herself as she watched him tip-toe past her, not even noticing her right there sitting on the couch. He went to the back room, but it was empty. *Now where the fuck this bitch at, with her slick ass,* he thought as he went to the kitchen and turned on the light, when he saw a person in the living room out of the corner of his eye.

"What the fuck?" he said, reaching for his gun.

"Yeah, muthafucka! Where the hell you been all damn night with yo' disease carrying ass? I hate you," Quies said, with her black .380 pointed at him.

"Girl, you better point that fuckin' cap gun someplace else before I put a hole in yo' light ass with this cannon. Fuck you talm 'bout?" Fresh barked pulling his .50 caliber from his waistline. "I been in the hood gettin' money, to answer yo' dumb ass question," he said as he emptied both his front pockets, dropping stacks of money wrapped in rubber bands on the table.

"Fresh, please. I don't want to hear that shit. I wonder if you was getting gonorrhea and chlamydia too because that's what I got when I went to the doctor today!" Quies responded with her pistol still pointed at him.

Fresh's eyes got big. He swallowed the lump in his throat. "Gonorrhea and chlamydia? You must got that shit from yo' other nigga cause I ain't burning!" Fresh lied with a straight face. A few days ago, he woke up to use the bathroom. While urinating, it felt like shards of glass were passing through his meat. The sensation bought tears to his eyes. He didn't know that he had infected her until now. He'd taken his antibiotics and assumed she was in the clear.

Tears ran down Quies's face and clouded her vision. "You can't even tell the truth. I gotta take all these damn antibiotics because you gave this shit to me!" she informed using the barrel of the pistol to point at the prescriptions on the kitchen counter.

"I'm sick and tired of you, Fresh, for real. All you do is lie, run the streets, chase bitches, and bring diseases home. I just found out that I'm pregnant with yo' damn baby and you do this to me. You're losing me and don't even realize that shit." She cried before lowering her weapon and collapsing to the floor.

Fresh walked over to her. He kneeled beside his woman taking her into his arms. "I'm sorry, Q. I fucked up, baby. I'll make it up to you. I promise." He rocked her back and forth her tears soaking his shirt.

"You having my baby. Why didn't you tell me?"

"Tell you how, Fresh? After they told me I had two STD's, I couldn't be happy about anything. Shit bittersweet. I'm happy and hurt," Quies admitted as a fresh set of tears wet her face.

Fresh kissed the top of her head. "I'll make it up to you, baby. I promise. I got caught up, drinking and getting high. I slipped. I promise it won't happen again."

Quies continued to cry. Allowing the bullshit, the man she loved told her to go in one ear and right out the other.

The pain in her pussy wouldn't allow her to forgive him that easily. "How can you make this up to me, Fresh? Thank God this shit is curable. It'll always be a different bitch, a different problem, a different drama. The fact that you had this shit and didn't think to tell me speaks volumes about your character. If I did that to you, you'd leave my ass after beating my ass!" she interjected, reading her man like a book.

Fresh could say nothing in his defense. He knew he was wrong but never intended to infect his lady. He loved Quies with all his heart, just had a fucked up way of showing it.

Fresh stood to his feet, picking Quies up in his strong arms. He carried her into the kitchen and sat her down on the counter. "I know that this won't make things better, but I want you take this. It's the least I can do. Start buying stuff for our baby and whatever else you want, ok?" He handed Quies one of the knots of money he had on the counter.

Quies shook her head. This was chump change and pennies compared to the heartache and trauma she endured from loving his thug ass. The meager money he handed her would never be compensation enough for the injuries done to a broken heart. "What's this, like five grand? Nigga, you make that shit in ah hour, so what you been doing the other ten hours? Nigga don't play with me. You and Major sell weight all day, and that's all you made?! Boy, please!"

"Now you countin' what I make?! Just play yo' fuckin position! Take the antibiotics to cure that shit, and everything will be cool. Getting on my fucking nerves with yo' ungrateful ass. Now what the fuck you cooked today? I'm hungry," he said as he looked in the refrigerator expecting to see a plate wrapped up waiting for him.

Quies hopped down off the countertop. A single tear made its way down her cheek. Her womanhood was dripping with pus and discharge, itching beyond comprehension, and he disregarded that shit as if it was nothing. "Nigga, you shoulda ate at the bitch house who gave you that hot box of gonorrhea and chlamydia! You better boil a few sausages or microwave one of them pizzas because I ain't cook shit! I ain't no fuckin' house wife, but don't worry. Soon as I get my ass up in the morning, I'm going down to Planned Parenthood to abort this damn baby. I ain't having a baby with a nigga that don't give a fuck about me." Hearing Fresh downplay the fact that he had given her two STDs infuriated Quies. If she didn't love him so much, she would've shot his trifling ass.

Quies stood 5'7, with flawless dark skin, and a banging body to compliment a gorgeous face. She put you in the mind of DMX's girlfriend in *Belly*, attitude and all. Just a lil' more ghetto like the one he had in the car sucking his dick. Quies did hair at Diva's Salon with her high school friends: Juicy Fruit, Ashley, and Terri. She did all the local dope boys and trap niggas' women's hair and stayed in everybody's business. She grew up in the Colony's Apartment Complex, but Fresh moved her to a house in Lincolnshire.

Fresh loved himself some Quies, but like most men, lust conceded to fidelity. Fresh didn't know how to show love. He had never seen his mother receive it. He grew up in Willow Run with a mother who worked long hours as a middle school bus driver to make ends meet. His dad died when he was younger.

The hustlers and hoodlums in the hood raised him, jeweling him to the game, but thanks to his partner, Major, life was always good. Fresh was about 6'2", 185lbs, dark skin, and wild as hell. If it wasn't for hustling with Major, he would definitely be a jack boy. Other than Major, his other idol was Maker, a local stick up boy from the hood. Maker, short for "meet your maker" was known to body niggas real quick. He didn't believe in murking or robbing guys from his hood, though, unless they got shit twisted or became disrespectful.

"While you pointing guns and shit, how bout count this fuckin' money, and putting it in the safe, and getting prepared to get fucked like you love it."

Quies reared her neck back like a snake about to strike its prey. "Fucked! Nigga if you put that burning, dirty dick anywhere near my irritated box, I will kill you," she spit with enough acid to sizzle his soul.

"I will count this bank though," she countered before snatching the money up from the counter and disappearing down the hallway to their bedroom.

She mumbled incoherently.

"What they fuck you say?" Fresh yelled at her back.

Quies ignored him, slammed the bedroom door, then locked herself into the room.

Quies knew Fresh was a liar and a cheater before getting with him. He kept his dirty deeds in the streets, never allowing her knowledge to the whores he slept with. She would never allow a woman to come between them. There wasn't a bitch walking this earth who could pry them apart, but diseases? Not one, but two diseases! They could not be forgiven. Not to mention, the itching and burning associated with the bacterial vaginosis nearly drove her insane. She shivered at the thought of wiping herself after using the restroom. "Every day, my feelings for him fade. He just don't understand how big the wedge is between us," she mouthed while separating the bills by denomination. Stacks of Washington's, Andrew's, Lincoln's, and big faced Benjamin's lay before her. "His ass is a means to an end. Soon as I get my own salon, I'm done with his ass. God just gonna have to forgive me for killing this baby, but I can't be tied to this nigga for the rest of my life. I can't spend my years laying with this nothing ass nigga who carries around diseases and fuck random bitches raw. Hell nah. He knew he had that shit and didn't even tell me. Low down muthafucka!"

Quies felt sorry for herself. She never wanted to become the type of woman who needed a man to boss her up. Yet, this was the hand she'd been dealt. The first time he cheated, she should've began stacking her chips. Stashing money away for a rainy day would've allowed her to make a clean exit. For the time being, she was going to tolerate whatever he took her through until she was set up in her own shit. Then, she might think of doing a little cheating of her own because she was long overdue for a new nigga who'd treat her right and pipe her with good, clean dick. Not the big, dirty dick that came along with Fresh.

Can't Stay Free For Shit...

"Fast livin' got me trapped in this street game. . . Before I die I hope I have a chance to make a change," Major rapped along with Master P's words as he pulled into the parking space at his PYT's apartment in Doctor's Circle. He'd been kicking it with her on the low for about two years.

He'd been calling her phone for the last thirty minutes but received no answer. He forgot to bring his key she gave him, and he was loaded with a quarter kilo of cocaine.

"Damn I forgot Majesty is at work," he said aloud as he walked to her backyard. He checked the bathroom window and the back door, but they were both locked.

"Man, I gotta get in this apartment," he grunted, growing frustrated. He needed to cook his work. Clientele awaited him, and the longer his work was in powdered form, the more money he'd miss out on. Then, he thought about it. She always kept her bedroom window open, just in case, so he went and checked it. It was open just as he thought. Major hopped through the window and headed straight to the kitchen to handle his business.

He was whipping up some fourteen grams of crack that resembled sugar cookies as they dried. He'd already put together ten of them when he heard someone entering the living room door. He went to see who it was and was shocked as hell to see Majesty's aunt Kisha stepping inside. He didn't have time to hide the numerous Pyrex jars filled with crack that lined the kitchen table.

"Fuck is that smell? Majesty, you in here?" Kisha yelled while walking through the small apartment sniffing the air.

The first place Kisha went was into the kitchen where she heard glasses clanking together from Major trying to place them in the Lim's bag he had on the floor.

Ding Ding. The microwave sounded off, signaling that the work was ready to be whipped. In that same moment, Kisha walked in. He and Kisha glanced towards the microwave at the same time.

"Oh, hell the fuck nah!" Kisha said. "I know good and goddamn well you ain't in my shit cooking no crack! " she yelled incredulously at the drug paraphernalia sitting atop the counters.

"Hold on, Kisha, let me finish handlin' my bitness, and I'm out," Major said.

"Nigga, you bout to get that shit and get out right now. Cause I don't know what you and Majesty got goin' on, but I ain't goin' to prison for you, so get that shit and get out. "

"Alright, let me call a cab."

"Nigga, you ain't waitin' for damn cab in here with that crack. I don't know what you doin' in here anyway when Majesty ain't home. Now gather up yo' shit and go."

"Hold up, Kisha, I respect you, but I ain't bout to walk the streets with this shit on me like that. Better yet, let me call Majesty. I thought this was her apartment. I pay bills in this bitch, and you ain't bout to make me lock my damn self-up."

"Yeah, call that bitch because this apartment in my name, and I ain't getting shit out the deal, so fuck what she say." Major hung up the phone before Majesty could answer.

"What you want then? I'll break bread with you Kisha; that ain't no problem, " he went into his pocket, peeled two hundred dollars off his knot, and handed it to her.

"Now, this what I'm talkin' 'bout," she said stuffing the money inside her purse. "Now, you may finish doin' 'yo thang. I'm bout to relax."

"Damn, you raised all that hell for nothing when all you had to say is to look out for you, with yo' money hungry ass," Major said as he re-heated his work. That was the last one he had to get right before he could make his exit. He took the other jars from the Lim's bag, then ran water into them. This allowed the cookie to not stick to the bottom of the jar. After allowing the work to dry for a little bit, he bagged it up. "Kisha, give me a ride to Willow Runs right quick."

Tsk. "You ain't gettin' in my car wit that shit." She plopped herself down on the couch and began flipping through channels dismissively.

"Fuck you too, then. It's all good." Major gathered his belongings after calling for a cab to come scoop him. After a few short minutes, he heard Blue Ribbon's signature horn toot outside.

Major slid into the backseat of the cab with a bag full of stones, ready to get paid heading back to the hood.

Margie handed Blade his daughter that he shared with Feebi and placed two turkey sandwiches on the table in front of them. She went back into the kitchen and returned with a small cup of juice for Ivory and a chilled glass of lemonade for him.

"Margie, I surely do appreciate you lookin' out for me," Blade thanked his mother-in-law before taking a seat on the couch in her two bedroom apartment in Gable Oaks.

"Blade, you got to leave Feebi alone, and do better for yourself. My daughter ain't shit," Margie informed, speaking ill toward the daughter she had raised. Never in a million years did she ever think Feebi would turn out to be a crack whore that sold her ass to get high.

"It's been a whole week, and me or you ain't heard from her yet. Heifer hasn't even picked up the phone to check on this here baby of y'all's. She got me here changing yo' bandages that she the cause of. Ivory don't deserve to be treated so bad. That girl needs to know that y'all love her, not the neglect she's been receiving since being born," Ms. Margie fussed.

"I know, Margie. Ivory gon' be alright as long as you around."

"You right about that, but this y'all child. Y'all gotta do better and spend some time with her. Shit, I thought I was done rearing cheerun. I'm up in age living off my dead husband's social security. I ain't got time for y'all shit. Ivory need to be in somebody's daycare learning new things and being around other cheerun her age, not my old ass."

"I know," Blade conceded, as he held his daughter combing his fingers through her pretty hair. "I know."

"No, you don't. 'Cause if ya' did she wouldn't be here with me every day watching *The Price is Right* and *The Young and The Restless*. Just take care of yo' self out in them streets. I know it takes time to fight that addiction, but you have to give yo' self a chance, Blade and stop letting Feebi control yo' life. You done let yourself go running behind her ass. Now you strung out, too."

"I know, Ms. Margie. I'ma pull myself back up."

"You need to go to one of those rehab places in North Carolina. Heard they get you back on solid ground and help you find a decent job." She supplied while rocking in her chair.

"I know about those places, Margie, but ain't none of them for me. Rehab didn't put me on drugs, and rehab ain't gone get me off of 'em. I'ma have to kick this habit cold turkey."

"Um hum," Ms. Margie mumbled. She'd heard that song sang before and didn't believe a word coming out of Blade's mouth. The only cold turkey Blade would kick was that sandwich he was fixing to bite into.

As they sat there having a decent conversation, the house phone started ringing.

"Hello?" Margie answered.

The automated jail recording played. "You have a collect call from "Feebi, an inmate at the Alvin S. Glenn Detention Center. To accept this call, dial one. To disconnect, dial two."

Margie pressed one. "Girl, why the hell you in jail again? You can't stay free to save yo' damn life."

"It's a long story, ma. I need twenty-five hundred to get out," Feebi answered.

"Now where am I gonna get twenty-five hundred dollars from, Feebi?"

When she said Feebi's name, Blade and Ivory looked in her direction. Blade missed her, even though she did him so wrong. The truth was, he wanted that old Feebi back. The one who wasn't mischievous, hostile, or getting high, but he turned her out. Now, he was paying for the flaws of her addiction. Feebi, though still pretty for a smoker, was once a bad bitch with a nice body, clear skin, and long, healthy hair that fell down her back. She strongly resembled Diane Carrol from the movie *Claudine*, but things had changed. She still looked good, but crack made her hateful, violent, and vindictive. She hated Blade for ruining her life. It was his fault that she was strung out on that shit. That was one of the reasons why she treated him so badly. Because although Blade got higher than a whore's mini skirt, he was able to function civilly and handled his habit much better that she did.

"Let me holla at her, Margie," he said as he reached for the phone.

Feebi really didn't want to talk to Blade, but she knew that he was her ticket out of jail.

"What's happenin', babe? I was wonderin' where you was at. How much yo' bond is?" he inquired. He'd come up with the money, be it hell or highwater.

Though Feebi hated Blade with a passion for being the cause of her addiction, one of his strong suits was always coming through for her. He held her down no matter her flaws. Blade never questioned Feebi when she found herself in trouble. He was always ready and willing to help her out as much as he could. "My bond's twenty -five thousand dollars, but you can go to a bondsman and pay ten percent," she explained.

"Come get me, baby. I miss you and need to get out of here before I start withdrawing, Blade. Please don't leave me in here," she begged.

"Alright, I know, baby. I'm on my way. You'll be out before night fall," Blade let be known before handing the phone back to Margie.

Margie snatched the phone from his grip and rolled her eyes.

"See, that's her problem right there. You always lettin' her have her way. She ain't gon' never learn her lesson with you always spoiling her. She rushing home to get that shit in her system. She ain't concerned about you or Ivory. While you wasting money on bull shit, you need to get yo' self somewhere to call yo' own and help raise yo' damn child."

"I know. I know, Margie," is all he said as he handed Ivory over to her and walked out the door to find a ride to get some money from the bank. "I'll see y'all later on."

Blade worked for a painting company with his homie, but he also did home improvement work on the side from time to time.

He tried getting a ride from his roommate, Cal, but he wasn't home, so he had Cal's next door neighbor call him a cab. Ten minutes later, a Blue Ribbon cab pulled up and Major hopped out the back seat. This was the first time they had seen one another since Major had left a knife in his back. They gave one another a quick stare down.

"Aye, what's up, Blade. I been meaning to come holla at you. Man, I apologize for stabbing you. Doing that shit didn't make me feel good. I was just under a lot of stress and took my anger out on you. Bottom line, I was wrong, and I hope you can accept my apology."

"I ain't sweatin' that shit, lil' homie, but we'll rap when I get back," Blade said.

"Cool! When you get back in the hood, come see me. I got some'n for you." Major finished holding a balled fist over his chest.

Blade returned the gesture before sliding into the back seat of the taxi.

*****

"See, those little niggas got this complex sewed up," the man informed while passing the binoculars to his partner so that he could get a better look. "The one in the white polo shirt seems to be the leader. That's who we'll follow first. I've been watching his set up for the past few days, which is how I was able to snatch his product a few days ago," he added.

"Um hum, I see that. I was wondering where you had gotten the dope from. There's a lotta drug dealing going on over here. Surprised the blues still not posted up out here since that shit happened to you," his partner responded while adjusting the binoculars over his eyes.

Brian grunted in distaste. The police department had all but given up on finding the perpetrator that left him hospitalized a few months ago. The incident had practically been swept under the rug because no one would come forward with information, but now none of that mattered. Brian chose to take matters into his own hands. Someone was going to pay for injuring him. He'd assembled a team of rogue cops to apply pressure on the city's "D boys."

"Keep watching the younger boy sitting on the steps. He's using that kid to peddle narcotics. Those hand motions he uses is a diversion for something. I've noted that every time he serves a fiend, he makes those hand gestures. One on the right, and one on the left."

"I hear you, Perry Mason. The girl too, she's in on it. I say, we hit the apartment she's going in and out of as well," his partner added. With a mortgage, new baby, and college to pay for his son, he was game for taking from who he considered scum of the earth to provide a better life for his family.

"Oh, no worries. We going in there, guns locked and loaded. I want everything these thugs have: money, coke, their life, or liberty, whichever comes first."

His partner whistled. "You's one cutthroat bastard, Steeples, but I like it!"

Brian stood from his squatting position ready to set things in motion. The police department failed to produce the person who had brought him harm. Therefore, he was taking matters into his own hands. Retribution. That's what he wanted. It was time for dues to be paid, and he didn't give a fuck about who was hurt in the process.

Lil' Punk Ass Niggas...

Major, Fresh, and Von sat on the brick wall as usual, doing what they do. They watched the white Altima pull up and park by building 15. Dude got out and walked in their direction. Fresh and Von put hands on their guns. One wrong move from this guy, and his noodles would be left decorating the sidewalk.

Major took a good look at the approaching man's face, then waved his shooters off.

"Oh, he good, y'all. That's my dog, Snail, from River Drive," Major provided. Von and Fresh concealed their artillery.

"What up, bruh?"

"You already know," Snail replied.

"Lemme grab two of them thangz you showed me the other day. That shit is glass and has the smokers on my line like bait!" Snail said as he handed Major his money.

"That's a stack."

Major looked over at the lil' boy who sat on Selah's steps in building 16 where a grill was burning. All day long, they'd been feeding whoever wanted a plate to create a diversion to hide the ultimate agenda of selling crack. Major held up two fingers on his right hand without Snail witnessing his move. The lil' boy went in his bookbag, took two crack cookies out, and sat them in one of the styrofoam containers that were conveniently seated next to him. He eased his way to the 15 building and sat the plate on the steps and quickly resumed his position back on the steps without Snail seeing him.

"Snail, you see that styrofoam plate sitting on that step over there?" Major nodded his head in the direction he was talking about. "That's you."

"Alright, bruh. I'ma get back at you later. Good looking out." Snail went and picked up the plate and headed to his car. Thirty seconds later, he pulled off, satisfied with his product.

While Snail was pulling off, a lil' girl around twelve years old came to the other side of the brick wall to get the money that was just made from Major and ran to one of the apartments in Willow Lakes (which is another project only over the brick wall from Willow Runs).

That's why Major chose to post on the wall to conduct his business. His twelve year old nephew, Petty, was schooled on how to handle the dope. When he hold up fingers on his right hand, it signified ounces. His left hand meant quarters. None of his customers bought less than a quarter, so things worked out easy and perfect for his nephew. Being that his sister's apartment in Willow Lakes was upstairs, Major paid his niece to watch when he made serves. She knew when her lil' brother made his move to await her signal. When Major knocked his bottled water over the wall, that was her cue to come get the money and take it to her momma. She carried every twenty-five hundred dollars made to the safe house.

Major's entire set up was fool proof unless you were within his circle. Only those close to him knew how he manuvered.

He operated in that fashion to ensure that his family was taken care of in case something he couldn't control occurred. His careful provisions allowed him to never have any drugs or money on his person just in case jackboys or the police came.

Fresh and Von handled all the cluckers. They sold pieces until Major left the hood. Daily, he hustled from noon to six. Then, Fresh and Von held the fort down from six o'clock to whenever, but being the sex fiends that they were, shop would close around midnight. Their pussy pondering allowed Mook and Big Ram to get their work off. No one could eat when Major was present. The smokers only wanted to cop from him because he always had premium product. His rocks were never stepped on.

As Major and his homies sat on the wall passing blunts of exotic back and forth, a cab pulled up, and they didn't like who was getting out of it.

"I don't believe this shit." Fresh said. "You see who got the nuts to show their faces round here."

"Shid, I ain't see her in bout a week, but he still be comin' through late night. He say he ain't holding no grudge," Von said.

"What's up, Major?"

"What's up, Blade?" Major said, as he hopped from off the wall and gave him some dap.

"You know me, just takin' it easy, lil' homie," Blade replied.

"Damn, Feebi! Where the hell you been hidin' at?" Von asked.

"I just went and paid twenty-five hundred to get her ass outta jail," Blade answered for her. "You know she stay in some shit."

"Yeah, a bitch had to slice a hillbilly trucker the fuck up at Flying J's last week," Feebi bragged.

"Ooh shit, that was you? I read about that shit in the newspaper, and it was on the six o'clock. You wild as hell, Feebi," Fresh said. He was not surprised because Feebi was known for being a crazy bitch.

While they were chopping it up, Feebi nor Blade saw when Major gave Petty the signal to put a quarter ounce of crack in a styrofoam cup and sat it on the step by building 15.

"Well, man, I hope we good, but grab that cup off the porch at building 15 on ya' way home and fuck with me sometimes."

"Alright, Major, I 'ma fuck wit you," Blade said as he grabbed the cup and kept it moving.

As him and Feebi headed to Gator's spot to get gaged up, he saw Mook, Big Ram, and a few females posted up.

"What's up, Blade? I see you still fuckin' with the same niggas who opened yo' ass up the last time," Mook said heading over to Blade and stepping directly in his face.

"You don't fuck with ya' boy unless you got short change? Wanna come spend with me when you got slot machine money, huh?" He slapped the cup from Blade's hand, but Feebi hurriedly picked the cup up from the ground.

Blade curled his top lip and gritted his teeth. "Nigga, yo' young ass betta chill. I ain't in no mood for the bullshit," Blade said as he slid his hand into his right pocket.

"Nigga, what you gon' do?" Mook pump faked in Blade's face. But Blade didn't flinch or bat an eye. That angered Mook who reared back, socking Blade in the face.

"Oh, hell no, nigga!" Feebi hollered, witnessing Blade stumble backward. She went over to help him get his footing. Blade was never one to back down. He couldn't let this lil' nigga make a bitch of him in front of Feebi. She would never let him live that shit down.
He quickly pulled his knife but dropped it by mistake from moving too fast.

"Damn!" he grunted as he attempted to reach for it, but Mook was already in motion.

Mook stepped on the knife. "Oh, you ain't ti'ed of pullin' knives on mufuckas?" He queried as he bent down for a split second to pick up Blades knife, and why did he do that? Mook should have never let his guard down. When he leaned down, Blade came out his left pocket with a switch blade and slammed it into Mook's head so hard that he fell to the pavement before bouncing back up as if he were on fire. The shock of being stabbed knocked Mook off his square. Blade wildly swung the switch blade slicing Mook's bicep and shoulder wide open. Blood oozed from his wounds saturating the oversized shirt he wore.

"That's right, baby. Poke the shit outta his ass. Fuck 'em up. Bitch ass, always messing with somebody!" Feebi hollered encouraging Blade to continue dicing Mook's ass up. Blade wielded the knife in rapid succession. Slicing away as if he were carving deli meats.

"Ooh, shit!" Mook hollered like a bitch as he staggered not to lose his footing. He took off running in the opposite direction. Hastily trying to get away from Blade with Big Ram trailing him.

"I told ya' don't fuck with me!" Blade yelled breathlessly while hitting himself in the chest. "

"Yeah, Major got me, but he only made me smarter mufucka. Y'all lil' young, punk ass niggas gon' learn to stop tryin' me. From now on, y'all mufuckas can call me "2 Blade". Come on, baby," he ordered, holding his hand out for Feebi to grab it.

Blade and Feebi left the scene while the bystanders cleared a path for them to walk through. Mook ran home like a wounded puppy with Big Ram on his heels. Neither one of them were gangsters. They weren't about that life. They fanned flames but couldn't tolerate smoke.

If This Ain't Some Bullshit...

Major pulled in the Copperfield apartments off of Broad River Road where he sometimes laid his head, and mostly stashed his money. It was a nice neighborhood; no drug activity or known violence, mostly college students lived there, so it was fairly a safe environment to live.

He parked in his assigned spot and walked towards his door and noticed it was slightly opened. *I know Kim ain't in my shit*, was his first thought, until he got closer and noticed it had been forced open by the chipped wood on the door frame. "Damn! If this ain't some bullshit!"

Major pulled his .38 snub from his shoulder holster underneath his Coogi jacket. He pushed the door open with his foot and peered into the living room. He quietly monitored each room to make sure no one was still inside. "Fuck," he uttered to himself as he noticed all of his shoe boxes gone along with the majority of his clothes. Empty hangers were scattered about the floor and left dangling in the closet. Right then, he knew that it was some petty thieves who came in his crib. Real jack boys didn't steal clothes and shoes. They wanted bricks, guns, money, and marijuana. Jewelry too, if that shit way lying around.

"Damn shame how petty they were to take all my fuckin shoes," he grunted, growing angrier by the minute. He kicked an empty shoebox against the wall. A single twenty dollar bill drifted from it, falling to the carpet like a leaf blowing in the wind. About twelve thousand dollars were stashed. He had two grand in the sole of the six boxes of Jordan's he had in there. That was money he had been saving up to cop his very first kilo.

"Oh, I'ma find the brave mufucka that came in my shit. Bet that. Let me call Kim," Major said, as he sat on his money green, velvet couch with his pistol on his lap. He lit a cigarette, then dialed Kim's number.

She answered on the third ring, "hey there my favorite cousin in the world. I was just talkin' bout you. You gone live a long time," she said, sounding all excited and boisterous as usual."

"What's up, cuz-o? Look, I'm at the spot and I need to see you ASAP!"

"Ok, see you in ten minutes."

By the time Major smoked another cigarette, she was walking through the door.

"Ooh, my God! Boy, what happened?" she asked, with her hand over her mouth.

"Shid, you tell me!" he said as he exhaled Newport smoke, looking at her waiting for a lie to leave her lips.

Kim stood in the door way stuck, lost in thought for a few seconds. "I know he didn't," he heard her mumble.

"Speak so I can hear you. My shit missing, and I want it back. What the hell you talkin' bout?" he stood to his feet and faced her.

"Major, I'm so sorry. Please don't be mad at me," she said while looking at him, knowing she had fucked up.

"Kim, I knew it had to be you because both my neighbors are barely home. When they are, those girls don't even have company, so what happened?"

"Damn!" she started patting her weave. "This morning I was running late, I forgot to check the mail box, so I stopped by here to get the bills to go and pay them. I wasn't thinking when I didn't drop Dip off first."

"Dip?! Lil' thieving ass Dip? You bought that roguish ass nigga to my shit?" Major asked incredulously. Dip's ass could steal the butter out a biscuit.

"Yep!"

"And how do he know you came to my spot?"

"I was on the phone with yo' momma when I was home and she reminded me to pay the light bill. We left the house immediately, so I guess he put the shit together. Right after we left from over here, he started acting impatient and rushing me to drop him off at his homeboy, Jab's house." Kim finished shaking her head and feeling like shit.

"Ok, now that I know he did it. Ain't no need in you thinkin' bout him no more. You ain't got no business messing with that bottom feeder no way. His lil' dusty ass probably gave you crabs." Dip would hug the block for days on end rocking the same clothes. Major was big on looking good and smelling fresh. He couldn't understand how niggas could go days without washing their ass and changing clothes. That shit was nasty and revealed a lot about their character.

"I'll kill that nigga if he gave me something, but I'm sorry Major. I moved sloppy cause I was rushing. Please don't be mad at me," she said, giving him the baby look while pouting.

"Too late for all that shit, just be prepared to get wit me later and show me his spots."

"Ok, but he don't be nowhere but in the Bishop."

"Alright, but I'll holla at you later, anyway. Call the office to see how much it's gonna be to break this lease. I can't live or stash here now knowing that those niggas know about it."

Major left Kim sitting on the arm of the sofa with her thoughts.

On his way back to the hood, he was lost in thought. He chain smoked Newport's. He craved a blunt of Loud but couldn't smoke that shit driving his mother's whip.

Major was supposed to be linking with his connect to re-up, but he wasn't in the mood to hustle. "I was so fucking close to copping my first brick. Damn those lil' niggas fucked me up!" Major banged his fist on the steering wheel out of frustration. He needed to cool down. His temper was boiling over. Major wanted to run up on Dip, put that cannon to his dome, and blow the noodles out of his spaghetti. But he knew he had to move smart and with a level head. He decided to stop by his sister's house to relax his mind and smoke a few blunts with his brother-in-law, Maker. He had devilment on his mind, and Maker was just the man he needed to see.

Major told himself that he was going to find Dip and send him and his goons on some capers to get his money back and extra, since they want to be robbing the robber. Major was also going to let Maker know that he was ready to team back up with him. It was time to pull those ski masks down and start back sticking niggas up in the city and wherever else money was to be taken. He was tired of hustling backwards. It was time he hit a few licks and started buying bricks. It was levels to this shit and robbing other niggas for their product would place him at the top of the totem pole.

He pulled into his sister's yard on Hardscrabble Road to see Maker sitting on the porch drinking a beer.

"Look at this nigga here. I can tell from your walk that you ready. Ya' look like you got it on ya' mind," Maker commented.

"What, nigga, you a mind reader now?" Major responded jokingly.

"Nigga, I know you. The game ain't showin' my lil' bruh no love? Nigga just say the word, and it's on. Shit, my stash done got low anyway."

"Well, nigga let's show up, and show the fuck out."

They bumped knuckles and Maker stood from his chair to get dressed. "It's showtime!"

Major pulled his 07' black Impala in the Bethel Bishop Projects and saw young hustling gangbangers posted in each section of the parking lots. This was Folk territory, but Major was on a mission. Them niggas knew Major's status on the streets. They weren't afraid, but they respected him. The majority of them copped work from him anyway.

His eyes focused on who he was searching for. He parked in one of the empty parking spots, watching the group of bangers through limo tint. He rolled a blunt of White Rhino and observed them making drug transactions. A dusty nigga on a normal day, Dip often wore the same clothes for days on end. The money stolen from Major's apartment made him bathe his ass. Today, he was dipped and dressed dope-boyishly in a black Nike jogging suit with silver, black, and green VaporMax covering his feet.

Look at this lil' nigga, done went to the mall and got fresh to death with my fuckin' money. I should run his ass over, he won't even see it comin', Major thought as he blew blunt smoke through the air.

"The niggas ain't even smart enough to see who's even in this car. Stupid, sloppy mufuckas! For all they know I could be the feds," Major flashed his headlights a few times at the group of dudes. They all looked but didn't know who it was, so no one made a move towards the car.

Major dialed a number in his iPhone. "Nigga, come holla at me right quick, this Major," he stated as soon as they answered the line.

"That's me. I'm blinkin' my lights at you."

"Nigga, get out the car and holla at me," Dip huffed with too much bass in his tone trying to act hard. He was tough as hell with his crew around. Inwardly he was shook as hell, wondering why he was there.

Major hung up the phone and got out of his car, then he sat on the hood to show Dip he was safe while smoking a blunt.

Dip ain't know what to think, but he knew the nigga wasn't dumb enough to try him in his own territory. Plus, Dip was sure that there was no way possible Major knew what he had done, so he decided to see what he wanted.

"What up, big cuz?" Dip said as he greeted Major.

"Ain't shit," Major replied. "Check this out though, I need you and a few of yo' most trusted soldiers to hit some licks for me."

"Shit'd, you know I'm with that. When you ready?" Dip asked, ready to go right then and there. Anything involving a lick was music to his ears.

"Get two of yo' most savage, thorough, brave hearted warriors together, and meet me at cuz spot in one hour."

"Say no more," Dip replied not knowing that he had just confirmed he'd been in Major's shit.

An hour later, they met up, and Major wrote down three locations and sent them on their way. While they went and hit the riskiest capers, Major and Maker hit a quick, easy one just to kill time until Dip called.

In New Castle, on Nancy Street, just like Maker's cousin told him, Spencer would arrive at his crib with a female around midnight. They rushed him as soon as he opened the door. Major grabbed the girl who screamed so loud, his eardrum vibrated.

Ack, Ack. She gagged as he gripped her neck choking tears into her eyes. "Shut up, bitch. Holla' like that again and I'll crush yo' mufuckin' windpipe."

She whimpered as tears cascaded down her face. Maker kicked Spencer in his back, knocking him over the couch, which was in the center of the living room floor. Maker was standing over him, gun trained at his face.

"Man, what y'all want? I got a few dollars. Just, please, don't kill me, man."

"Aight, let's get that change then, nigga." Maker said.

Spencer got up from the floor and started walking toward the back bedroom with Maker behind him, gun to his head. Major tied the female up and had her face down on the living room floor. He sat on the couch with his foot on her back, waiting for Maker to return with a bag of money.

While in the room, Spencer opened the doors to the walk-in closet. He kneeled down, removing several shoe boxes. The carpet had been cut out, and beneath it, a small hotel sized safe sat face up in the floor.

"Don't be brave, nigga. Try some heroic shit and ya' family will be selling plates to bury yo' ass," Maker warned, but Spencer wasn't stupid. He shook like a stripper with the barrel pointed at his dome. He opened the safe with no hesitation, revealing bundles of rubber band bank.

"Man, this all I got in here," Spencer provided as he pulled the money out of the safe. "This sixteen thousand dollars. All I got to my name. Just don't kill me, bruh."

"Stand up and turn around. Take one of those pillow cases off the bed," Maker ordered, jamming the barrel harshly into the back of his victim's head with so much force that a small gash opened. Spencer rushed to the bed nearly tripping over his own feet.

"Slow mufucka. Don't make me cap yo' scary ass."

Spencer slowed his steps removing the pillowcase as instructed. Pellets of sweat dripped down his bald head. Spencer continued to shiver as if the room were freezing cold.

"Squat down, and put the money inside," Maker watched as Spencer closely followed his orders.

"Now, back to the living room, nigga."

Once they entered the living room, Major was smoking a blunt with his foot still resting on the female's back as she laid flat on her stomach on the floor.

"Ok, bruh, he's all yours," Maker said. "Oh yea, he came off of a few stacks for the team."

"Alright, big timer. Where the dope at and don't fake because our sources already told us what we need to know. I just wanna give you a chance to show yo' loyalty. Talk to me, boss," Major said, jokingly chambering a round just in case Spencer decided to play stupid.

"Man, damn! I got a half of key buried next to my dog house."

"Let's go and get it, and don't try no slick shit because you and that mutt will die."

While Major had Spencer take him out back to get the dope, Maker put old girl in the hallway closet and sat a chair behind the door knob, locking her inside. He could hear her sniffling through the door. "If you make a sound, if I even hear your ass sneeze, I'ma shoot through this door. You hear me?"

Maker received no sound from the other side of the door. "I said, do you hear me?"
"Y-y-yes! I hear you," she stuttered. He ventured into the kitchen opening and slamming cabinet doors shut. Finding what he was searching for, Maker grabbed the loaf of bread off the countertop and opened the refrigerator, snatching the ham and cheese off the shelf to make a sandwich. After throwing it together, he bit into it as he walked outside to see how things were unfolding with Major.

An angry pit bull barked aggressively as Maker approached. Foam oozed from its mouth; he wanted to get loose so badly. He looked like he'd eat their asses alive if given the chance.

"Shut that canine up before I make a throw rug outta his ass."

Spencer snapped his fingers and patted his thigh, silencing the dog who sat on its hind legs wagging its tail.

"What he had back there, bruh?" Maker inquired while using his finger to remove the sandwich fixings from the roof of his mouth.

"Half a key and a few ounces," he responded, shaking the dirt from the Crown Royal bag the work was in.

"Now this is what I'm talkin' bout. I love when a plan comes together," Major opened the bag and held up several single bagged ounces concealed within a zip lock bag. Major then walked over to the dog and stabbed it in the neck. They took Spencer back inside the house, locked him in his hall closet also, and left. "We should've bodied they ass, bruh. Fa' real," Maker regretted not putting his murder game down.

Major objected. "Nah, bruh. We ain't gotta do that shit. It's already hot as a ho's pussy out this bitch. If we can help it, we'll never catch a body unless it's absolutely necessary. Ya feel me? Niggas not calling the police because somebody came in and snatched that dope. But we get to dropping bodies, and that's going create cases. We tryna be free while getting this money." Major wanted to boss up and get bread, not move sloppily and catch cases.

"You right, bruh. Your way of thinkin' makes a lotta sense. Mission accomplished."

As Major and Maker sat in his sister's driveway smoking blunts and splitting their profit, Major's phone rang. He looked at the caller ID. It was Dip calling.

"Yo, what up lil' cuz?" "Where you want us to meet you at?" Dip asked.

"Come to my apartment," Major replied.

"What apartment?" Dip said, not knowing what direction the conversation was heading in with Major. "You talkin' bout Kim's?" He asked playing the dumb role.

Major kissed his teeth. "Nigga, don't play crazy! I'm a boss, nigga. I ain't sweatin' the minor shit, just meet me in thirty minutes."

"Alright, cuz, and man...I'm sorry for the situation," Dip apologized meaning every word because he didn't expect Major to know what he had done.

"Nigga, like I said, thirty minutes. The money you 'bout to be makin' is worth more than what you got from my spot, so don't worry bout that small change. I'm on my way."

"Alright, I'll be there."

Maker looked over at Major curiously. "That shit sounded real crazy. You need me to roll with you?"

"Nah, it's all good and nothing I can't handle. That nigga is nothing but bait for some bigger fish we'll fry. Trust me, but I'll hit you later. Let me go settle up with these niggas."

Major and Maker bumped knuckles before Maker got out of the car.

Major pulled up to his apartment to see Dip, Jab, and Alley sitting in a sky-blue Chevy. Major got out of his car and walked over to their whip. Dip was happy to see he was alone. He started not to come, afraid that Major was going to have Maker, Fresh, or some of his other goons black bag his ass. Greed caused him to take his chances.
"Y'all get out, and come in," Major demanded.

As they entered the apartment, Jab's guilty conscious had him uneasy and paranoid. Major quickly picked up on his anxiety.

"Nigga, sit down and relax." Major said. "If I wanted y'all dead, I coulda crept up on y'all wit no problem in da Bishop, but I'm bout to help y'all get stupid paid while y'all help me. You niggas got heart, and I figured, why kill y'all when we can make money together?"

"That's love, cuz-o," Dip said, happy to be included in Major's plan. "Man, I'm sorry. It's just that it's hard out here. Ain't nothing but table scraps being thrown my way, and I'm tired of that shit. I want a full course meal."

Major respected Dip's honesty. He was hungry himself and understood the lil' dusty nigga's plight.

"Well, let's split that money and keep our dealings on the hush. Y'all need to learn how to make noise without doing a whole lotta talkin', if you following my drift. Don't go fuckin' up y'all money either. No showboating. That shit just draws unnecessary attention. Be smart. I got licks for days, so be ready and lay low," Major eyed the group as everyone nodded their heads in agreement.

"Say no more," Dip added.

They counted the cash from the three capers. When they were done, each walked away with ten grand apiece and split one and a half kilos, some weed, a few guns, and some jewelry. That was more dope and money than either of them had ever seen.

"Like I said, don't spend y'all money on cars and bullshit. Y'all got enough work, so put the money in the stash like you ain't got shit. Look out for y'all other homies with the dope, and if y'all listen and follow my lead, I'ma make y'all rich."

They all agreed to move inconspicuously. Major always had the aura of a boss, so they all assumed that he was already paid. Little did they know, he would use their backs to step on in efforts to elevate himself. Truth of the matter was, Major was just as broke and down on his luck as they were. He just made his brokenness and lack thereof look easy. Major was about to take over the city. With lil' niggas on his team, he could dominate the game. They were Folk gangbangers and had a big squad backing them whenever enforcements were needed. Not to mention, his lil' brothers who were in the Blood gang over in the North Main, Fairfield Road, and Broad River areas. He had plans to unite all the city's gangs, stop them from beefing with each other, and have them focusing their energy on getting money. It was about to be on.

Gutta Bitch...

Major decided to take Selah to the club to relax his nerves and scope out some possible licks. Dope boys loved the strip club atmosphere. It gave them the opportunity to ass watch and trick on pussy while stunting and flossing at the same time. It was still early. The sun was out and shining brightly. The temperature was just right at seventy degrees. It wasn't too hot or too cold. The perfect weather to enjoy a few drinks with his ghetto queen and scheme at the same time.

As they posted by the bar, Major could see all the niggas watching Selah and Triece (Von's girl), but Von was booed up. He didn't peep the same game Major did. Day in and night out, all Major had on his mind was elevation and envisioning a come up. Selah would be the perfect female to use as bait and was always with the shits. She and Major had been playing this game for years, using Selah's honey to attract the bees of the trap. She loved when he was on this type of shit. More money for the both of them. Plus, she loved the thrill.

"Baby, peep how dude wit all the platinum jewelry keep watching me. What you want me to do?" she asked Major.

"Handle yo' business. If he ask, just tell him I'ma average Joe Blow, lame as fuck, payin' yo' bills. You know how we do, but go have a few drinks with him, and get that nigga number."

"I got this, boo," she said, as she strutted towards the restroom.

Major noticed dude glance over at him before following her. Once out of view, Major could see him talking to her through a few mirrors that decorated the walls.

"Yo', sexy, let me holla at ya' real quick."

"What's up?" she replied licking her lips to lubricate the lies. She oozed sex appeal with a dancers physique and gapped, bow legs that looked as if she'd been horseback riding all day.

"I see you, and I like yo' style. Tell me you can get away or is that your man posted at the bar?" he inquired using his head as a compass to point in Major's direction.

"I do what I wanna do. He ain't really my nigga. Just a square trying to fit in my circle. I'm in search of a new sponsor," Selah informed cutting to the chase. She was about her money and didn't want this nigga thinking otherwise.

"If you bout' that same shit, let's talk. If not, don't waste my time."

"Well, in that case, what's yo' name?"

"Shay, what's yours?"

"Geno," he said, as if he ran the city. "Let's have a few drinks, sit down, and get more acquainted."

"Yeah, we can do that. Let me use the restroom first though. This drink is running through me."

Selah faked like she was using the bathroom but texted Major and told him the deal. When she came out the restroom, Geno was waiting for her. Geno followed Selah over to the bar where Major was seated with his chest poked out as if he was doing something. It took everything in Major not to burst out laughing from this clown ass nigga's antics.
"Aye, boo, I'm gon' have a few drinks wit my friend, ok. I'll see you in a minute."

"Alright, enjoy yo' self," Major said, switching his voice to sound like a lame and giving Geno a friendly head nod.

Von and Triece both looked at Major with suspicions. "Just some nigga we bout to rob," Major replied to their curious looks.

Fresh saw Selah sitting with dude and automatically knew that Major was back up to his old shenanigans. Fresh was too caught up in Quies and Trina lately to know that his homie had resumed strong arming niggas, bitches too if they were connected to some work. Major started back making niggas get down or lay down and wasn't going to force Fresh into his way of things. Once he saw the new level Major was on, he'd definitely want a piece of the action. Doing g-shit was right up his alley.

"Aye, bruh, I see y'all, and you know I was waiting on you to get back on that level. If you need me, I'll be in the parking lot handling some business wit Trina," Fresh said looking like he was clucked out of his mind.

"Yeah, I hear you," Major replied.

*****

Ack! Ack! Trina gagged from Fresh choking her as he rocked her boat in the reverse cowgirl position. She forcefully slammed her ample bottom back matching his strokes. "Yes, baby. Get this pussy, daddy."

"Shut up and keep ridin' this dick fa me!" Fresh choked her harder putting more force in his stroke, pounding her as if he were being paid to do so. His balls slapped against her monkey as he drove himself in and out. The sounds of their skin slapping together sounded like a pit bull drinking water.

Uh! Uh! Fresh grunted to stifle a moan.

Her head continuously bumped the ceiling of the 77' Chevy Impala as she grinded around, side to side, and up and down, all in the same motion on Fresh's long, thick, jet black, and crooked love muscle. The "Rod of God" is what he called it.

The car appeared to have hydraulics as their sex session caused it to rock and sway. Shit like this turned Trina on. She was really enjoying the thrill of sexing the thug she loved outside of the club. Watching the ass and titties of the dancers in the venue had gotten the both of them so horny, they had to come outside for a fuck break.

"Uh-uhn! Where you goin'? Don't run from the dick," Fresh said, as he grabbed her by the shoulders, pulling her down on his Rogerwood sausage simultaneously rocking side to side, hitting her tight walls and plunging into her bottom.

"Goddamn, boy! You all the way in my fuckin' ribs. Stop hittin' my shit so hard! I hate when you pop them damn Blue Dolphins because you be tryna kill a bitch wit that hook dick you got," Trina said as she caught the dick from every angle he threw it at her.

"Shut the fuck up. You love this rod, don't you, bitch? Don't... nobody... fuck... this... pussy... like Big Dick Fresh, huh? Huh?" he asked as he fucked Trina like it was going to be the last piece of pussy he ever had.

The x pills had them humping like wild animals and sweating as if they had just ran a few miles in one hundred degree weather. Their sexing had the leather seats sticky, Trina's weave clinging to her forehead, and the windows were foggy and wet.

Fresh roughly pushed Trina off of his lap.

"What you doin', boo, you ain't even nut yet?" Trina stated wanting to make sure that she had pleased her man. She tried pushing him back into the seat and straddling his lap, but he wasn't having that.

"Hell, nah I ain't finished! Turn yo' sexy ass over. I'm bout to make confetti of that pussy right quick," he said, getting up to position her in doggy style as he laid his seat all the way back.

"Nigga, you already got me sore, better be glad it's still wet, or I'd make yo' big dick ass pull outta me." Fresh had his left hand gripping her small waist, while he rubbed his meat up and down her pussy and asshole. The pills had him mugging, sweating, and gritting his teeth all at the same time. Nigga resembled a geeked up Bobby Brown the way his mouth was cocked to the side.

"No, no, hell no. You ain't putting that hog leg in my ass, boo. I want it in my pussy. She's beggin' for you to slide back in her, daddy. When you put that big monster in my tight wet pussy, slap my ass cheeks real hard like you do when you're mad at me. Ok, daddy? I want you to spank meeeee, OOOOWWWW! Trina said in pain as Fresh rammed his dick in her asshole anyway.

"I told you no, baby," Trina objected. Her body stiffened as he invaded her rear.

"Shut the fuck up and take this dick wherever I put it."

Mmmm, Ooh, Trina's objections quickly turned into moans. Fresh moved his hips in a circular motion, opening her ass cheeks wide to accommodate him.

"I knew you liked this shit. Damn, you so tight, gonna make a nigga bust too fast. You like how all this dick sliding in yo' tight asshole, huh? Don't daddy fuck you good?"

"Yeah, daddy."

Fresh eased his stick out of her, then rammed it back into her warmness. "Ooooh, shit," Trina hollered throwing her ass back while Fresh moved behind her like he was dancing to a reggae beat. His eyes rolled into the back of his head. His nuts tightened, it felt as if all the blood in his body had traveled to his penis. Trina felt his thick tool jerking around inside her. She clenched her sphincter around his love muscle while squeezing his nut sac at the same time. "Baby, I'm cumming all over this big dick. Yes, baby. Give it to me," Trina moaned.

The movement sent him over the edge. Fresh sped up his thrust, determined to spill his seeds all in Trina's ass. He leaned over her shoulder, kissing her on the neck, face, and sucking on her earlobe while slow grinding Trina's asshole making sure she got her nut and saturated his meat.

He then took it out her ass, entered her wet pussy and pounded into her slimy, thick juices for ten minutes straight.

All you could hear was moaning and groaning. They were sweating so badly, the driver's seat and the back seats were soaked. Even though the windows had tint on them, you could still see the fog on them. Fresh flipped Trina on her back, he let the seat back up, and put both her legs in the air, feet to the ceiling. He had his fists balled up, with his knuckles on the seats beside each of her ears in push-up position while stroking that pussy from every direction possible, hitting all her corners, walls, bottoms, all in her rib cage, stomach, and chest. Fresh was trying to catch his nut, but he was too clucked up and numb.

"Goddamnit baby, please. Let me suck it. You killin' me," Trina begged feeling her womanhood drying.

Fresh was so zoned out, he forgot where he was, what he was doing, and who he was doing it with, until he got tired of stroking. He pulled out of her and stood over her on his knees. Sweat poured from his body. His breathing was rapid. He was geeked up, higher than giraffe nuts.

Trina chuckled. "Damn, baby, you beamed the fuck up, looking stupid as fuck in the face."

He looked down at Trina. She was looking up at him as if he was a possessed demon. She was clucked out also, with her hair all sweated out, mouth twitching and mugging just like Fresh.

"Shut the hell up. You ugly as a mufucka right now, too. Damn mouth cocked like a pistol and shit," they stared at one another before bursting into laughter.

Fresh opened the back door and got out butt ass naked in the club's parking lot, big dick still on swole. He had completely forgotten where he was at until he saw security standing at the front entrance of the club.

"Fuck y'all looking at? Never seen a long dick before?" he joked, mimicking Kevin Hart. Other people looked over in his direction but didn't say anything because they already knew Fresh was a loose cannon. Fresh got back in the car, but in the front seat. Trina climbed in the passenger seat from the back, pulled her dress down, and rolled a blunt.

"Here baby, smoke this so you can come down a lil' bit because yo' ass is clucked to the max." She handed him the spliff then reached between his legs and started putting his boxers and pants back on him. Nigga was too high to do so himself. If he bent down, his ass would tip over.

"That's why I can't stop fuckin' with you girl. We be gettin' tweaked and havin' some of the gangsterest fuck sessions, fa real!"

"I know, baby. Shit be feeling so good," Trina sat at an angel before ducking her head to take Fresh's semi erect Johnson into her mouth.

His eyes were closed, enjoying the euphoria from the weed filling his lungs. "Got-damn, baby. Fall back off that dick for a minute, damn. You a junky for this dick. Here, get this blunt, and calm yo' damn nerves."

Fresh zipped his pants and tucked his stiff dick away from Trina's dick hungry ass.
Trina kissed her teeth then punched him playfully in the arm "remember that shit the next time too, nigga!"

Fresh mushed her in the face, then connected his phone to the car's Bluetooth.
You my gutta bitch, who I'm with when I'm in shit wit my other bitch, my other bitch when my other bitch on some other shit. Like ole girl, I need you to keep my Majesty.
Webbie's *Gutta Bitch* filtered through the Bose speakers as he and Trina rapped along with the southern rapper. Fresh eased

the car out of the parking lot heading towards Trina's house, so they could finish what they had started.

Chance Encounter...

As Major pulled up in the hood, he hit the accelerator and swerved in the back of the 16 building and hopped from his Cadillac STS in the middle of the parking lot blasting Plies' *36 Oz's* while rapping. "A nigga don't wanna see me wit that thirty-six, but a nigga gon' know when I get that thirty-six... thirty-six ounces, nigga that's a whole brick and I'm one flip away from gettin' a thirty-six," Major rapped as he stood in his opened car door, bouncing around in a hyped manner

"Nigga, you off the chain!" Fresh said.

"Nah, nigga, after we sell all that free coke I got stashed, we really gon' be off the chain. If I could get you and Von to stop fuckin' with these hoes and fuck with me on all the niggas I been robbin' lately, we'll really be paid, but keep bullshittin', and watch how quick I elevate. I got dreams, *Millionaire Dreams,* straight up!"

"I feel you, bruh," Von said while sitting on his 77' Chevy with the 24-inch Snipers.

"Nah, nigga, you gon' feel me when y'all see all the work' we got and all the cash we bout to count. Think it's a game, it's on now. All we need is a connect."

"Nigga, you always talkin' 'bout buyin' bricks and havin' millions, but niggas from the hood don't become millionaires. When you gon' let that pipe dream go?" Fresh said.

"See, that's where you're wrong. All I dream about is being rich, my nigga, and dreams come true. Thoughts become things. When you know better, you do better, you live better, you eat better. If you learn to save yo' cash and stop ballin' before you get it, you'll understand why a nigga think on such a large scale. A nigga getting rich right under yo' nose and you still don't see the big picture. These streets got yo' head fucked up for real, but a nigga like me tryna be just like my name says, Major! Don't worry though, just because you my nigga, I'ma take you to millionaire status with me. Just roll with me and continue to have my back and I'ma show you that hood niggas do become rich."

"Nigga, I can't wait to see some of this coke you got because I ain't see you this happy and crunk in a long time. Shit, go and get me some right now, and let's get rich then, " Fresh said.

As they were shooting the shit, the fucking city police pulled up and threw the lights on Major for the loud music and illegal parking. He still had his car in the middle of the parking lot.

"Damn!" Major said as he walked to his car. He just remembered he had a blunt in his ashtray.

"Don't move, sir. Stay where you are, both of you," he ordered, halting Major's steps. His partner followed him out of the patrol car and approached Fresh.

"Arms out, legs opened," the other deputy instructed. Fresh assumed the position. Having been frisked and locked up countless times, he had no problems assuming the position because he knew that he had nothing on him. But something about the officer questioning Major seemed familiar to him. He just couldn't put his finger on it.

"Are you driving this vehicle?" he asked with authority.

"Yes sir, I was just feeling good about my new born daughter. I bragging to my friends how happy and proud I am," Major said, hoping he could talk his way out of a fucked up situation.

"Well, sir, congratulations, but we got a call about loud music. You're in violation of the noise ordinance, and is that marijuana I smell? Reach inside the car and hand me your license and registration," he said.

"Spread your hustle and find you somewhere else to go," the other officer who was frisking Fresh instructed. He released his weapon from the belt then walked around to the passenger side of Major's car with his firearm pointed.

Fresh sucked his teeth and proceeded across the street, but not too far that he couldn't pay attention to what they were doing. He pulled his phone out and began to record just in case a problem popped off. A small crowd had formed to see the drama unfold.

"Sir, I hope that's not a blunt in the ashtray?" The officer on the passenger side asked opening the car door to retrieve the blunt from the middle console.

Major thought about trying to snatch it up right quick and eat it but wasn't close enough to do so. Besides, he knew better than to take his chances and risk his life. The media was filled with trigger happy, crooked cops waiting to shoot a black man down.

"Damn, can y'all just write me a ticket? That's a joint. Like I said, I was only celebrating being a first time father. Cut a brother some slack."

Neither of the officers paid his plea any attention. Major peeped the stoic expressions on their faces. They didn't give a fuck about him. His ass was going to county, period. The officers weren't trying to hear anything Major had to say. All they were concerned with was making an arrest. Far as they knew, he could've been the one who assaulted their fellow officer a while ago. They were still mad about not finding the person responsible. They handcuffed Major, took him to jail for illegal parking, loud music, and possession of marijuana.

"We'll be down there to get you in the morning, bruh," Von informed.

"Nigga, this ain't shit! Trust me when I say that this is the last time a city will be able to ever touch me for some petty shit. I'll see y'all tomorrow. Get ready for the good life."

Major sat in the Alvin S. Glenn Detention Center sitting in booking for the last two hours watching tv and tripping off the drunks and crackheads, but it was a Mexican who couldn't make contact his people who caught Major's attention.

"Don't look defeated, man. What you need, a three way call?" Major asked when the Hispanic man took a seat next to him.

"Me not remember number," he responded in broken English. "Dem muthafucka take me phone with all me numbers."

Damn! Major thought to himself. "What you in here for, if you don't mind me asking?"

"Me? Driving, no license. Me come to this South Carolina for one day and look what happen. Me just leave hotel getting rest. Me drive me truck from Texas, and all me family numbers in me phone."

"Check this out, man. When we go to court in the morning and they give us our bond, I'll get you out of jail, ok?" Major said feeling good. His spirits were still high at the thought of executing his plans when he got out.

"Do that for me, and me will look out for you. Me have lotta moneys. I take care of you, my friend," he added reassuringly.

Major shrugged his shoulders. This Mexican looked far from rich. It looked like he'd been outside all day selling oranges from the tattered clothes he donned and the busted boots on his feet. His face was unshaven and hair disheveled. Everything about his ass was popped. Major wasn't the least bit convinced.

"Don't sweat it, man. On my word, I'll get you out tomorrow with me. I promise."

"Ok, my friend," the Mexican smiled revealing platinum fronts while extending his hand to Major. "My friend, me name Miguel. What's yo' name?"

"My name Major," he replied, and as they were introducing themselves, their names were being called.

"Andre Major!" the C.O. yelled.

"Yeah?" Major replied.

"Miguel Garcia!"

"Si?"

"Si, my ass. Line up against the wall and grab a mat," the C.O. instructed.

"Come on, Miguel. We gotta change clothes and go to the Y-Dorm. We can use the phones and get some rest back there."

"Ok, my friend, me rolling with you," Miguel replied.

They got dressed out and were escorted to the dorm, and just their luck, they were also put in the same room. They talked all day. Miguel instantly took a liking to Major. He saw how everybody knew and respected Major in the dorm, and that made him a little more comfortable with being around him.

"Miguel, walk over to the phone with me so I can let my people know that she got to pay yo' bond in the morning."

With no hesitation, Miguel followed Major to the phone. Major made the call to Selah, and the next morning after the bond hearing, Major and Miguel were being called for release. Miguel couldn't believe how some dude he just met looked out for him like that. He was more than grateful for Major's show of compassion.

Miguel had Selah take him to North Main on Oakland Avenue across from the Wing Basket. Miguel introduced Major to his family as his new friend. Major chilled for like thirty minutes then he pulled Miguel to the side and told him he had to leave. It was like fifty Mexicans in the yard getting lit and lifted just enjoying themselves. Major rode past them every day, and all he ever saw them do was drink. They seemed to be alright people who minded their own business.

"My friend wait one minute. Me have to pay you back," Miguel suggested, sincerely.

"Nah, Miguel, we cool. I did that from the heart," Major said, as he placed his right palm over his heart.

"My friend at least leave me yo' phone number, so we can hang out and get to know each other, maybe have some drinks over lunch or dinner. Talk about some serious business, for real. I really like you. Hold on, let me get something to write yo' number, and give you mine," Miguel said as he attempted to walk in the apartment.

"Hold on, I left my phone in the truck, but I got a pen," Selah said. She went in her purse, wrote Major's number down on a piece of paper, then handed it to Miguel.
Miguel and Major shook hands and Major walked to the truck. Miguel stood there watching Major's swag. The way Selah moved when he moved informed him that Major was somebody very important in the city.

"Baby, I think that Mexican want to give you some work," Selah said, as they headed to the hood in the all-white Tahoe Major had bought her a few weeks ago.

"That wetback ain't got no damn work, but I'll see if he calls. Until then, I got a good bit of product I need to move," Major informed as his phone vibrated on his hip.

"Watch and see, baby. I'm telling you. He has the keys to the city. I can smell it on 'em."

"Yooo?" Major answered weary of the unfamiliar number.

"Major, my friend. Me wanted to make sure this the right number. Listen, me will call you in the morning. I need to talk to you about something serious. In the morning, answer yo' phone, my friend," Miguel demanded.

Major looked over at Selah, then he took the phone away from his ear and looked at it. "I'll be waitin', my friend."

"Who was that, bae?"

"That was Miguel, and he wants to give me that work for real. I can hear it in his voice. He said he wanted to holla at me 'bout some serious business."

Selah danced in her seat. "I told you! Them mufuckas need the blacks to move all that coke they got. It's on now, babe!" she grinned slapping the steering wheel with glee.

Khalid Ain't Got All the Keys...

At nine o'clock the next morning, Miguel called as promised. He had his people chauffeur him to pick Major up, and they went to a restaurant named Garcia's on Percival Road.

As they sat at a private table in the back of the restaurant, Major noticed how Miguel was treated. He sneezed, a Kleenex was bought to him, and once they were seated at their table, a five course meal fit for a king awaited them. The staff catered to him like a Don. Every five minutes they were asking if he needed anything. He said something in Spanish, and they didn't come back around for the remaining of their meal unless he motioned for them.

"Check this out, Major. Me like yo' style. You have a good heart. What you did for me proves that you are a decent man and that your word is bond. Men with sustenance these days are a rarity. I recognize boss potential and loyal characteristics. I also saw how dem at the jail love and respects you. I am a very wealthy and well-connected man. I have all the cocoa you could need or want. I'm not gon' beat around the bush with you. You looked out for me, just so happen, you helped a big boss. You didn't have to do that. I didn't need for you to do that, but for your services, me will compensate you greatly. Major I want you on my team. I want to help you become a rich man. What do you say?"

Major's heart hammered inside his chest. This was the big break he'd been hoping for, but he didn't allow his anxiousness to show. "Miguel, as long as you treat me fair and never play me, I'm with you."

Miguel made a phone call and two minutes later, a bulky Mexican who looked more Samoan than anything came from the back of the kitchen with a black brief case and sat it on the table between Miguel and Major.

Miguel opened it halfway so Major could view what was inside. "This is ten kilos of pure fish scale pericol. For you, fifteen grand a-piece. I give you one week. You play fair, me give you what you want."

Major whistled as his eyes danced across the purest product he'd ever seen. "Say no more," Major replied as he reached for the brief case. He was more than overwhelmed but did his best to conceal his excitement.

"Let me go, so I can get this money. This is all I was waitin' on, a good connect."

"Just don't fuck me, Major," Miguel warned giving Major a look that let him know he was powerful and serious about his money. But the look Major returned let Miguel know that he was a killer also.

"I'm a man about my paper who also wants to eat. I got you as long as you got me," Major replied. They shook hands and the deal was official.

Major sat in the plush break room of his cell phone and computer store, Major-Way Communications, watching the news.

It was just coming on. *Good afternoon, this is WachFox News. A robbery occurred earlier today at Tate's Pool Hall on Fairfield Road. Jabar Tate was shot and killed. He died at the Richland Memorial Hospital. His father, Jessie Tate, also sustained gunshots wounds, but is expected to survive. Witnesses stated that armed men entered the establishment donning army fatigues and ski masks. A dozen other people were also present during the incident but were not injured. If you have any information about this tragic situation, please contact Crime Stoppers at 803-888-HELP. I'm Joan Fields, over to the weather forecast.*

"Look at these stupid niggas, done killed Jabar!" Major said to himself. "I hope they got that money and dope, though."

"Major, what the hell you thinkin' bout?" Kim asked, snapping him out of his thoughts.

"He needs to be thinkin' about opening that other phone store in the Summit like I asked him because a phone and computer store in that area would do really well."

"Everybody up that way is financially stable," Majesty said as she walked in.

"If that's what you feel will be a smart investment, the money is already in yo' possession. Make it happen," Major replied. "For real, Major?" Majesty asked, sounding very overwhelmed.

"Do yo' thang. Kim, you just have to hire some more help."

"That ain't no problem. We already got everything in order," Kim informed.

Major got up and walked in the front of the store and noticed it was raining like hell outside. That's when he remembered he had to get to his brother's girlfriend, Monique's house, ASAP.

"Damn! I'ma holla at y'all later," he said.

"Oh, no you won't, either. Come here. Let me holla at you in private real quick." Majesty demanded with her hands on her thick hips. Major halted his steps. Majesty never demanded anything from him. She was easy like Sunday morning and went with whatever wave he was riding.

"I'll let y'all chat. Major, hit me up later," Kim stated stepping in to hug him before she disappeared into the next room.

Majesty waited for Kim to close the door behind her before strutting over to Major with her lips poked out. She folded her arms across her chest with her head hung low.

"What's up, babe? Why you acting like that? What is it that you need me to do for you?"

"I don't ask you for nothing, Major, but you've been neglectful as fuck. I barely see you unless it's about business."

Major pulled Majesty into him wrapping her in his embrace.

"Oh, so this is what yo lips are poked out for? You miss me?"

"I miss you, babe, a lot. You haven't held me like this in weeks. I need your affection, crave your kisses, need for you to apply pressure within my intimate parts," she provided looking him squarely in the eyes.

Major tilted Majesty's chin upward and he leaned down and kissed on her soft lips. "I'm sorry, baby. I got you. I promise. A nigga been busy as hell."

Major sat Majesty on the desk then raised her dress before pulling down her panties. He licked up and down her meaty thighs, nipping at them delicately with his teeth as he neared her flower. Major parted her wet lips with his fingers. Her nectar coating them with silky wetness. He slipped his middle finger into her tight crevice as he nibbled on her pearl.

"Ssshhh" Majesty hissed like a snake, enjoying the tongue lashing Major afflicted upon her clit.

"That feels so good, baby. Suck this pussy. Make me cum, baby. Please," Majesty worked her hips in a circular motion matching the movements of Major's tongue and fingers. She moaned loudly with her head tilted backwards.

She opened her legs wider, placing one hand on the back of Major's head to push his face further into her wet box. Her nectar coated his face, dripping down his chin. Majesty arched her back and humped her ass off the desk as Major continued to suck on her clit and finger all in the same motion. "Cum for Major. Cum on my tongue, babe," Major encouraged as he sucked harder, inserting one, two, and then three fingers into her dripping wet tunnel.

Major lapped at Majesty's center like a thirsty Rottweiler. He felt Majesty's body shake as her juices continued to run out of her like a raging river. Major drove his fingers into her rapidly making the *come here* motion inside her and knocking against her G spot. Her thighs did a nervous twitch before she wrapped them around his head and shoulders grinding that clit into his mouth.

"Dre, I'm cumming, baby. Oh, my gawd, I'm cumming baby," Major drank her juices as they flowed endlessly from her center. His face resembled a glazed honey bun. Shiny and sticky from her sweet juices.

Major stood from his squatting position. His dick was missile hard as it fought to escape the confines of his denims. He didn't realize how badly he needed to enter her body until now. Her pink, hot, and wet pussy was just the distraction he needed from ripping and running in those streets. He hurriedly unbuckled his pants, allowing them to fall down and around his ankles.

Majesty played in her monkey awaiting Major to give her what her body craved: fast, slow, hard pipe from the only man she loved. Major moved her hands out of the way so that he could glide his stick up and down her slick opening. He teased that pussy, putting the head in then taking it out. "Please, babe. Give it to me. Let me feel that big dick." Majesty begged in a sexual zone. Major slid his dick up and down her crevice once more before entering her tight hole. Her womanhood held him in a vaginal head lock. His dick felt like a knife cutting warm bread as her pussy enveloped his meat.

Majesty bit her bottom lip, her eyes rolled into the back of her head. "Damn, Majesty this pussy feel good as fuck!" Major complimented before slamming his Johnson inside her. He was balls deep, slamming his bat repeatedly again and again. He pounded her pussy. It sounded like he was stirring a hot pot of macaroni as her pussy sounded off. *Clap! Clap! Clap! Pop! Pop! Pop! Clap! Clap! Clap! Pop! Pop! Pop!* They were in a zone trying to make up for lost time and the many days of him not pleasuring her.

Major drove deeper and deeper with all his might. The stapler, pencils, pens, and the keyboard all flew off the desk as they got it in. Majesty squeezed her vagina around Major's tool, milking his pipe. He sucked her titties, taking each nipple into his mouth as she popped her pussy against him. He felt her pussy percolate and knew that she was about to bust again. Majesty loved when Major sucked her titties and pounded her pussy at the same time. "Do that shit, baby. Aww, baby, yes. Yes! Fuck this pussy, baby. Beat it the fuck up!" she encouraged smacking him on the ass. Major galloped in the pussy. Majesty raised her hips then slammed them down onto his pipe over and over again. The tingling between her legs intensified. Majesty raised herself onto her forearms, kissing Major aggressively in the mouth before dipping her head and taking one of his nipples into her mouth. She flicked her tongue then reached down between them to put her index and thumb about the base of his dick forming an O. "Gotdamnit!" Major grunted going faster and faster and pounding into her as hard as he could. Majesty continued flicking her tongue over his nipple and neck feeling his dick jump and thump within her body. "Fuck me, baby. Fuck me hard. Just like that!" Majesty panted breathlessly.

"Oooh, shit. Yes, baby. I'm cumming, cumming all over that dick. I miss this dick so much," she cried as orgasm after orgasm took over her body.

Majesty's walls sucked him in. With each pump he threw, Majesty squeezed his meat until he spilled buckets of semen into her body. Major collapsed on top of Majesty, licking her nipples and kissing them at the same time. His seeds continued to spill inside her while she grinded her pelvis against him. "Fuck, girl. You just had a nigga feeling like a whole bitch."

"I'm supposed to make you feel good, baby. That's for keeping the dick away from me all those days, nigga," Majesty playfully mushed him in the face.

"Oh, you definitely did that," Major leaned down and kissed her on the lips before pulling his wife beater over his head and wiping off with it. He helped Majesty down off the desk, and she walked into the bathroom and returned with a warm washcloth to wipe him down.

"Thanks, baby. You don't know how bad I needed to feel you, Major. I missed you like crazy. Don't ever keep my dick away from me that long again."

"You swear you run shit, don't you?" Major asked before kissing her again.

"Nah, you run shit. I just follow yo' lead."

"And that's why I love yo' lil' black ass."

Major kneeled down to pull his pants up. He went into his pockets and removed a stack of money placing it in Majesty's hands.

"Go get yourself something nice, baby. I promise I'ma make time for you in the next few days. Ok?"

"Ok, I'ma hold you to it. Thank you, baby, and be careful. It's raining lions, tigers, and bears outside right now," Major kissed Majesty again then headed to his car, running to avoid being soaked from the pouring rain.

On his way to Greenview Estates, he thought about how far he'd come. With the help of Kim and Majesty, business was booming within the phone store. He remembered after buying his very first big eight of cocaine, he gave Kim a grand every week until he had more than enough to open up the store, and now, without even using the money from all his robberies or the work he got from Miguel, Majesty was ready to open another store with some of their revenue.

That just goes to show how much progress they had made. He, Kim, and Majesty made good business partners. With their help and assistance, he was on his way to having a chain of MajorWay Communication stores.

Major pulled up in Monique and Wayko's yard. Wayko was one of Major's lil' brothers who hustled for him in the Gable Oak apartments, or wherever he felt like getting money. He had a reputation for busting his gun, so niggas in the city respected him and his other homies space.

One of the head Bloods in the city, he represented the GKB Bloods, who mainly dwelled in the Broad River Road, McDuffie Street, the Colonies, and the entire North Main area.

Major dipped into the backyard and dug up the half kilo of cocaine he had stashed before entering the house through the kitchen door.

"Damn, bruh! Look at this shit," he said as he held up the bag which revealed nothing but yellow liquid. "This was a whole half of brick of one solid block of fish scale!"
Wayko and two of his Blood homies walked in the kitchen where Major was getting the Pyrex jars from the cabinet.

"Damn, bruh, what you bout to do with that shit? It ain't nothin' but water now," Wayko said, thinking Major had lost out.

"Nigga, watch how a veteran put the hocus-pocus on this shit. Nigga, daddy taught me well. Just check me out, nigga," Major bragged as he poured a lil' bit of the liquid from the zip lock bag into all of the Pyrex jars. Then he added some baking soda and more water to them and microwaved each one for two and a half minutes.

"Bruh, what you doin'?" Wayko asked fanning the air. Though profitable, the smell of cocaine cooking gave off a terrible aroma.

"Nigga, I gotta test the weight off the eye, but watch this shit, my nigga. This ain't nothin' but coke that got wet; I've been through this shit plenty times. I told you I'm a vet, nigga, a true, die hard dope boy."

After a few hours of transforming the liquefied coke to crack, Major had the crack cookies looking nice and thick like always. He fronted the work to his brother and his two soldiers for unbeatable prices. "Y'all make some shake off this shit. I got a lot more when ya' finished with that pack."

"Fasho, bruh. We bout to shake the block. Got nuttin' but pieces for the pigeons! Good lookin', bruh. A nigga about to get full and fat round this bitch now."

Them niggas suited up in their rain suits and boots, then headed to Gable Oaks to get that money. Major was impressed by their grind. He left right behind them because he had work to do and big boy moves to make.

Lil' Wayne's song *Money On My Mind* played as Major smoked a blunt of White Rhino, riding, thinking about all the money he was about to stack. He couldn't believe how well life was treating him. He decided to go out to the club so he could let the city's brick layers know he had *them* thangs for cheap, but he headed to the hood to holla at Mook first.

He walked into his dad's apartment to relax his nerves. His thoughts had been never ending since coming in contact with so much product. In a way, he didn't know how to handle it all. The money was steadily piling up. Coming back to the hood allowed him to remain humble. When he entered the apartment, his dad, Blade, Feebi, and his stepmom were in the living room drinking Seagram's Gin and smoking crack. Major spoke, then took a seat at the kitchen table to roll himself a blunt to get his head right. Major had the crib nicely laid out with pretty, baby blue furniture, matching curtains, and a 50" Plasma TV. He had to make sure his younger siblings were comfortable. He didn't care about what the parents did. As long as his siblings were good, he was happy.

Major called Mook and told him to come to his dad's spot, forgetting all about the incident that had occurred between Blade and Mook.

"Major, you must forgot that Blade just gut that soft ass nigga?" his dad, Gator said.

"Oh yeah! I forgot. 2 Blade ain't no joke," Major said, holding his hand over the phone. "Mook, just hold tight. I'll be to you in few minutes."

Major walked in Mook's mom's apartment. "Bruh, I ain't gon fake with you, I got more work than I can handle. You been playin' fair from day one, and I want to put you on brick status if you with it."

Mook's eyes bucked at the offer. He couldn't believe what he was hearing. "Hell yeah, my nigga! When do I start? You know I got clientele all over the city."

Major went in his waistline and came out with a whole kilo. Mook's eyes grew big, not believing that he was touching his very first brick, and from Major, the dude he thought wouldn't amount to shit. *Damn I wonder where the fuck this nigga get a brick from.* Mook considered while holding the block in his hand.

"Mook, you play fair, and I'll keep you supplied. Let's do square business and get money. I'm plugged in. My nigga, it's time for niggas in our hood to outshine the city. Let's get it."

"How much, bruh?"

"For you, twenty-four grand," Major replied taxing him. The price of kilos had inflated since the feds were in town. At thirty grand a pop, Major stood to earn bank from consignments alone. Besides, he knew Mook was about to get all he could off the brick, being greedy.

"Alright, bruh, get at me. I got plenty more, so move that shit fast, and move up. Get yo' money. Stack yo' chips. You feel me? I'm out."

He was on a money mission. Flooding the hoods with quality coke at unbeatable prices.

Major then sold two kilos to his old connect, Rico, at twenty grand a-piece, making those birds fly. "Nigga, I'm proud of you. Khalid ain't got all the keys. Look at'cha moving whole thangs and shit now."

"It's nothing, bruh. Whole lot more where that comes from. Fuck with me though," Major and Rico dapped up before parting ways. He wanted to believe that Rico's sentiments were genuine but knew otherwise. Niggas wanted to see you doing good until you were doing better than them. That's when the hate and jealousy started. Major just hoped that, for Rico's sake, he wouldn't attempt no funny shit. After parting ways from Rico, Major sold out of all the work he had within twenty-four hours. Miguel fronted him twenty this time, and in two days, it was gone. He was getting fifty kilos within two weeks of meeting Miguel.

Even Fresh had stepped up. He and Von had taken Major's position in the hood. Petty and his niece missed helping out in the hood. He had them doing other things now. His niece and Petty managed and counted his money. He did that just to keep them a part of the team and give them something to do.

Major still hung in the hood but not as often, only when he wanted to relax and chill with the homies. Business was booming, and he wasn't able to sit still due to all the bricks he slang.

Major headed to Fresh's new house he rented in Meadow Lakes to pick up some money. He hopped out of his STS dressed in a green and white velour customized 803 sweat suit, matching fitted cap, and some all-white Van Grack's on his feet. When he walked in the house, Fresh had two Spanish chicks sitting on his royal blue love seat couch; a red bone in his recliner, and a brown skin chick on the floor next to the red bone. Major spoke, then walked in the kitchen where Fresh and his boy Vito were at the table, counting money, smoking a blunt.

"What up, bruh?" Fresh greeted.

Major wasn't happy with the way Fresh was handling his business. "Why you doin' this in front of them females? This ain't a movie. This street shit ain't scripted, homie."

"You already know how I do, bruh! But we bout to get that orgy poppin' in a minute. You want in?" Fresh offered not even acknowledging Major's point.

Before Major could reply, one of the Spanish chicks said some slick shit out her mouth. "I ain't suckin' hood rat pussy. Ghetto cat can't sit on my face," she mumbled loud enough to be heard.

"Hood rat? Ghetto cat? Bitch, y'all ain't gotta get down with us! Y'all bitches can beat the pavement if you ain't fuckin," the red bone fussed standing up with fist balled and nostrils . flared.

Both Spanish females started talking shit in their native language. "In this house, we speak English. Speak so I can understand yo' taco eatin' ass!" Red bone stated walking up on them with her fist balled.

"I said," she was silenced with a closed fist to the mouth that busted her lip. Red bone slugged her in the face repeatedly while the other female with her attacked the other Spanish mami. Fresh sat back and laughed. Major just shook his head, knowing that all the drama was bad for business. They let the girls go at it for a minute, just for some good entertainment, then they broke it up.

"Oh, that's how you gon' play it, Fresh? You bring us over here and let us get jumped on?" one of the Spanish chicks said.

"He should'na let y'all bitches come around anyway," Brown skin said.

"Don't worry though, I'll make sure to show my peoples where you rest your head at," the thickest Spanish chick said as they walked out the door.

"Yeah, you crossed the wrong senoritas, papi," the other Spanish chick said as she slammed the door.

Fresh ran to the door and yelled, "send 'em, please, so I can burn 'em. Bitch, I ought to put a hot one in ya' ass for threating me."

"You want us to finish what we started? I'm always game for beating those bitches. They kill me thinkin' that they better than us," the red bone asked, standing up ready to run them down.

"Nah, I got some'n else planned for them," Fresh replied snidely.

Major grabbed the money off the table and stuffed it inside his 803 tote bag. "Bruh, I'm out. Y'all got too much going on over here. You need to get a new spot; You can't trust those broads."

"I live for drama, my nigga. You already know how I get down. I ain't running from them *esses*. Those wetbacks bleed just like I do!" Fresh boasted.

Major threw his hands up and hauled ass. There was no use in trying to talk reason into someone who wasn't trying to hear it. Beef would need to be tenderized from fucking with those bitches. Major could taste it.

He told his other female friends he would get at them later, then he walked out behind them and got in his grey

Durango. The girls lived in the neighborhood. He didn't offer them a ride because they lived around the corner.

Fresh and Vito rode through the hood searching for the Spanish girls and spotted them walking towards the exit of the neighborhood. As they approached, they could overhear the thicker one speaking rapidly and loudly into her phone.

"Oh, she heated, Fresh. Bet that bitch on the phone sicking her people on yo' ass right now," Vito provided knowing how devious and cutthroat women could be when they felt jaded.

Fresh pulled beside them. "Why y'all left the house like that? I apologize for having ya'll around them lame hood bitches. I shoulda known better because they ain't on y'all level."

"Yeah, you got that shit right, papi. That shit was not called for," the thick one agreed.

"Papi, we don't go through shit like that. It was real ghetto of them to start some bullshit with us," Slim added.

"Y'all, get in the truck and let's go grab some'n to eat. Plus, I got a few dollars for y'all to show my gratitude."

They looked at one another exchanging knowing looks. The slim one wanted to object, but she wouldn't leave her friend. They came together, so they'd leave together.

"Thank you," they quickly hopped in the back seat, happy they didn't have to walk any further.

Vito rolled another blunt while Fresh hit the highway driving an hour outside of the city. He got to Augusta, then pulled out his shit.

"Y'all burrito eatin' bitches, get out my shit!" he ordered, shifting the pistol from one female to the other. The girls' eyes bulged as they looked at one another, mouths agape.

"Go on, git, bitch! Run those phones, too, goddamnit," reluctantly, they handed him their phones.

"Ok, ok, papi. Easy," the thick one stated, sliding across the leather seat to exit the truck.

"Now y'all hoes can walk back. Never check a real nigga, check a hoe!" Fresh hollered before speeding off. The tires burned rubber and spit gravel and dust in the females' faces as Fresh drove off, leaving them on the side of the road. "Why you doin' them like that? We shoulda at least fucked them pretty ass hoes first," Vito said.

"Because, those quesadilla eating hoes threatened to have us robbed. That's a valuable lesson to teach them not to play me for a sucker. I'ma fuckin' gangsta. Now let 'em do the shit for real."

"Boy, you one dirty ass nigga," Vito said, laughing.

"My nigga, I'm from Willow Run Projects, and we don't take no shit from no hoe, and I still ain't moving outta my house. Fuck what Major talkin' bout! I want them hoes to send somebody over there, so I can embalm a nigga."

Heartache... Hair Loss and Herpes

Walking to her black BMW SUV, freshly off of work, she decided to call her boo to see if he would have some drinks with her later. Kimiko was a fifth grade reading teacher at Brennen Elementary. She lived in Lake Carolina (one of the wealthy, elite sections of the city). Her father is a Dean at Allen University, and her mother is a petite Asian lady who owned and operated a day spa. Kimiko had given birth to a son who was now two years old during the time Major wasn't coming around too often. She met Major at their insurance company three years ago. Over the years, they had managed to maintain a good friendship, but lately, they've been spending a whole lot of time together.

Major hated the fact that she had a baby with someone else. A street nigga, and a young one at that, settling down and raising a family wasn't on his agenda at the time, but he still had love for her and accepted her son. He was the one who'd become distant, forcing her to move on with her life. Kimiko's mixed heritage gave her an exotic appearance. She had that skin tone that appeared as if she was always on a beach, honey roasted and tanned year round. She was slim thick, weighing in at 130lbs with silky, curly hair that draped down her back when straightened.

At twenty-five years of age, Kimiko had it going on and was on her way to being very successful in life. She had her shit together. Whenever he went to her home, it was always well maintained. Her credit was good, and she hadn't been ran through by the niggas in the city. All good qualities that Major preferred in a woman, but he refused to be secondary to her baby's father. She didn't have him on child support, so that alone let Major know that, if given the chance, the father of her son would be right back in the picture. Kimiko was the story book type and wanted a family, so he wouldn't allow himself to get too close to her or attached.

"What's up, baby?" he answered.

"Are you going to be busy around seven, because I want to take you to a bar and have a few drinks? Pleeaase! I really miss you," she expressed, meaning every word.

"Ok, babe. Just call me when you're on the way."

"Thanks, honey. See you then, I love you, bye!"

"Love you too," he replied meaning every word.

Major liked the experience of dealing with her. She never did the things he was accustomed to like eat and shop in the same typical places all the time. She enjoyed experiencing life and all it had to offer. It was the same with her though; she liked going to places he knew about. They took turns exposing one another to their usual hang outs. He never had to pay for anything when with her. She didn't need anything he had; she came fully equipped and didn't need upgrading. She had her own and he loved that.

He enjoyed being taken away from his average dope boy world. Even if it was only temporary. Being around her was comforting and changed his daily routine.

Major was the eldest boy of his mother and father's kids. His father had children spread out all over the city. Major had six brothers, all a few years younger than him, and five sisters, all younger, except for the one who had kids by his boy, Maker. His oldest sister, Sonya, was Crystal and Petty's mom. She practically raised Major; that's why they were so close.

Major stood 6'2", 200lbs, and wore his hair braided to the back. Niggas round the way loved clowning him about his braids, calling him "Pusha T" and shit, but fell silent when they learned that their bitches liked running their hands through them. He could pass for Terrence Howard's twin, but don't let the good looks and hazel eyes fool you. He was a stone cold gangster, just like his father, Gator. Gator's a heavy crack smoker who used to terrorize the city in his dope boy and jack boy days, but don't sleep on him because he and Blade still lurked and pulled capers on that old school shit. Apples didn't fall from the tree, and all Gator's sons were thorough street niggas who got it how they lived.

Even though Major's family wasn't wealthy, and he had to grind to survive growing up, he still didn't judge Kimiko's spoiled ways, but sometimes he grew a little impatient with her complaining. Overall, he loved her.

Seven o'clock rolled around quickly. Major had Kimiko to pick him up at the Majik Market across the street from Willow Lakes. He kept her on the low. Selah knew about her, but he didn't want other people in the hood to know about her. He believed in keeping certain things and people confidential.

When she called his phone and told him she was five minutes away, Major jumped the brick wall from Willow Run Projects, over to Willow Lakes apartments and walked to the store. As he crossed the street, she admired his swagger and dress code in his Crown Holder denim jeans, white and blue Creative Recreation shoes with the double straps, his Crown Holder sweater, and NY Yankee fitted.

Major swaggered toward her BMW truck with his bowlegged trademark walk with a half a blunt of Purple Thrax. He slid into the passenger side, taking a few extra pulls from the blunt before he thumped it in the parking lot. He had one foot in and one foot out as he blew the smoke into the air. He got in the truck, and they met each other with a passionate French kiss.

"Major, what did I tell you about smoking that stank stuff before you got with me?" she huffed in bougie dialect.

"Girl, cut it out! Just let the windows down for a few minutes," he replied, not up for her whining.

She reached in her side door and handed him some Gucci Guilty Intense cologne for men. "I bought that just for you. You're going to have me and my truck smelling like Purple Thrax, and I know my parents are going to ask a million questions. Gosh, Major! Take off that sweater and throw it away. It smells like you've been smoking hay all day."

"Girl, you've gone crazy for real now! I ain't taking off shit. You can drop me back off. You always complainin' when you know how I roll. You a grown ass woman with a child but you let yo' folks treat you like a one. I'm my own boss, and I do what I wanna, when, and how I wanna, so if you can't deal with me the way I am, I guess I ain't the one for you to be dealing with. Cause ain't nann woman bout to tell me what the hell I can and can't do."

"Ahh, boy hush your mouth. You know you're my sweetheart. I guess I can stand a little contact," she said in her proper tone while rolling her eyes.

"Boy? You best check that shit too, cause I'm all man. You gone learn how to speak to me. You've been fucking with a nigga for too long for me to have to educate you on how to fuck with me," Major said as he reclined his seat to enjoy the ride.

"The next time we do something together, you gon' have to ride wit me in my shit, so you bring some extra clothes because it's gon' be some blunt smokin' and gangsta music bangin' all through my whip. No negotiations, you dig?"

"Understood, sir."

"Like I thought."

Major and Kimiko sat at a table in the back of Alligator's Bar & Grill conversing and sipping on their third double shot of Grey Goose and cranberry.

The drinks had Kimiko feeling real good. Just looking at Major admiring his thuggish, pretty boy features was creating a puddle inside her panties. He watched a white couple dancing with no rhythm; they seemed to be in their own world.

"Major, have you ever thought about settling down and having kids?"

He turned around and faced her, wondering where that question came from. "When I meet that special someone and the time is right, why?"

"What do you think about me?" she queried, wanting questions answered that had been nagging at her for weeks.

He looked her in the eyes and grabbed her hands, caressing her knuckles with his thumbs, "baby, you are a very sweet and intelligent person whom I would love to take seriously, but your mind is stuck on having a life with your baby's father. I can tell you're still in love with him, and I won't ever interfere with your love for him. He's given you something that I haven't, and I won't compete with that. I love spending time with you, and I know you love me but is not in love with me. I know that I'm really not your type because yo' parents expect you to marry someone with high standards. Someone who has a college education and wealthy parents like them. I can't help it that my daddy is a crackhead, and my mom's boyfriend and I don't get along. This is my life, and all I can do is live it the way I know how, so until you're tired of me, I'm here."

"Major, I love being with you. You're right about my parents, but you've opened my eyes to the simple things in life. When I'm in your company, I can be myself. Unfiltered, without you passing judgement. I know you have other women who love you, but I want to remain as a fixture in your life in whatever way I can. And you're correct, I really wish I could make things work with BJ's father, but he's a loser and I can't make him see what I see in terms of a monogamous relationship. He thinks he can pop in and out of our lives, but I'm sick of him. But I want us to spend more time together, ok? Please, be patient with our friendship, Major. I love you," she finished as tears welled up in her eyes.

"I got love for you, too, but don't expect me to wait forever," Major glanced at his vibrating phone on his hip.

"Ok, Major. Thank you."

He grabbed it from his swivel clip and observed the caller ID, not familiar with the number, but he answered anyway.

"Baby, excuse me, I'ma take this call."

"Do your thing, sweetie," Kimiko responded.

"Hello?!"

"Major! This is Quies. Fresh has been shot!" she yelled into the receiver, barely audible. "We're at Richland Memorial."

"I'm on my way," he said and hung up, then he turned to Kimiko. "Baby, I need for you to take me to the hospital, my partner has been shot."

With no hesitation, she grabbed her purse and they walked out of Alligators to her truck, which was parked directly in the front parking lot. On the way to the hospital, he couldn't stop thinking about the conversation he had with Fresh regarding those Spanish girls. Intuition told him that they were responsible for Fresh being shot.

When he and Kimiko arrived at the hospital, Quies and Fresh's mom were in the waiting room crying hysterically.

"Major!" Quies yelled as she ran to him falling into his open arms while crying on his shoulder. "My baby was shot six times," she cried, breaking down with each word she spoke.

"Where he got shot at?" Major asked "Is it real serious?"

"He's alright. They got him in surgery right now. Some girl got shot too."

"What girl?"

"I don't know, but I wish I knew because I would go and whip her ass while she's laid up with bullets in her ass. I'm trying to find out, but they won't tell me shit," Quies admitted through bloodshot red, tear stained eyes.

Kimiko sat back and listened. *Damn, she's ghetto. Who would want to fight someone while they're already suffering from an injury? My god, are these the type of people Major associates himself with?*

As they were in the waiting area talking, the doctor approached. He pulled the paper cap from his head before speaking. "Do you all belong to the Drake family?" the doctor inquired before speaking.

"Yes, we do," Ms. Drake answered standing to her feet to hear what the doctor had to say.

"Well, Ms. Drake, the surgery was successful. No vital organs were hit. Phillip lost a lot of blood requiring a blood transfusion, but all is well. He's expected to make a full recovery from his injuries though he will be very sore and stiff for several days, possibly weeks, as his body heals."

"Thank you, God," Ms. Drake started speaking in tongues, thanking the God she served that her son would be alright.

"Can he have visitors now?" Quies asked anxiously.

"Yes, he may have visitors, but take it easy. Don't bombard him too quickly. He's under sedation but has been speaking," the doctor informed.

When they walked into the room, Fresh was propped up in the hospital bed with pillows behind the right side of his back, so the left side didn't have any pressure on it. The left side of his body was heavily wrapped in white gauze. He looked like the Pillsbury dough boy and had so many IVs and tubes running from his body that he resembled a science experiment.

Quies ran to his side. Kissing him all over his face. Concern and worry gave her a haggard appearance. Her hair was disheveled and looked like she had stuck her hand in a socket. Dried tear stains streaked her face. "Thank God, you're going to be ok, baby. I thought I lost you."

Fresh kissed Quies before turning his attention to the other visitors.

"What up, y'all?" Fresh said, smiling as they walked in his room.

Everybody spoke, then greeted him individually.

His mom had a disappointed looked on her face, "Phillip, I hope you leave them streets alone, baby and find yourself a job," she said.

"Ma, I was at home when some dudes kicked in my door and shot me."

She sucked her teeth. "I bet they were looking for drugs and money," she stated knowingly. She knew what her son was involved in and didn't mince words with him.

"Them niggas had the wrong house," he lied, but she knew better.

"Phillip you might can tell these people standing in here that sack of bullshit, but I ain't stupid. Don't piss on my good shoes and tell me it's raining. You ain't gon' stop until I'm standing over yo' cold body at the city morgue. Don't you want more for yourself? You run the streets committing all types of crimes like you don't care if you live or die. You need to tighten up son and get your shit together."

Fresh dropped his head as his mother chastised him. His mother was having church exposing his truths, but he wasn't trying to hear any of it. Her words entered one ear and exited the other.

"Well, since I know that your mannish ass is going to live, I'm leaving. I ain't going back and forth with your ass about the shit you doing when you know you're bringing it on yourself," Mrs. Drake walked over to Fresh planting a kiss on his forehead before exiting the room without uttering another word.

Once his mother was out of the room, Major spoke openly knowing that Fresh wasn't lying about someone kicking his door in. "I told yo' ass to be on your game after that bullshit went down the other day at your spot. You don't listen, man. Them damn Spanish girls," Major uttered just above a whisper so no one else could hear what he said.

"I know, bruh, but I'ma get those hoes back. Mark my words. To be honest with you, the way those niggas moved was calculated as hell. Real talk, and between me and you, I don't think it was those Spanish bitches."

This nigga tripping. Must be the drugs that has him talking outta his head. "You don't think the Spanish girls have their hands in this? You pulled a cutthroat move. You know those bitches are revengeful."

Fresh shook his head and stared off as if he were reliving what transpired all over again. "Because, bruh, they were synchronized, moved just like the police. The way they came in the house, separating and searching the rooms told me they had done that shit before. If it was over those mamis, I would've been left stinkin'. You feel me? If they wanted me dead, I would be. They took the dope and money I had in the spot. That's what they wanted."

Major ran a hand over his face at that revelation. He didn't know what to think as his mind ran rampant. A million scenarios went through his mind. *Who are the Spanish chicks connected to? Is Fresh running game on me because he's fucked up his package?* He wanted to press Fresh for more details but decided against doing so. Too many eyes and ears were in the room, and he didn't feel comfortable having a conversation pertaining to coke around Kimiko's prim and proper ass.

"We gon' kick the shit as soon as you get outta here. I'll get you back right on that other thang too. Just get yourself well. Heal up, bruh."

Fresh and Major bumped fists before Major started towards the door with his hand on the small of Kimiko's back. Before he could exit the room good, he heard Quies showing out and going off.

Quies marched over to the bed with fire and rage in her eyes. "Who was the bitch who got shot?" Quies asked getting in all up in Fresh's face.

"That was Vito people," he replied lying.

"Whatever, but Vito wasn't there, huh?" she asked. Quies talked shit until she grew tired. She wanted to know who the female was that had taken bullets alongside him and when hospital personnel refused to tell her, she decided to leave. She wanted to kill Fresh. He'd taken her through too much bullshit for him to be keeping secrets. She was sick and tired of being sick and tired. Loving Fresh only brought heartache, hair loss, and herpes. She held onto their relationship because she knew that no one else would want her once they learned that she carried an incurable disease, but since she'd been taking the antiviral medication, Valtrex, as prescribed, she hadn't experienced an outbreak in months. "Why me, Lord! Why am I so fucking stupid? The minute his ass showed me he couldn't act right. I shoulda left. Now I'm stuck with this disease that he gave me, and he's still running around spreading that shit like its ok," Quies continued the conversation with herself.

She was devastated when she woke up one morning to use the rest room only to have her panties glued to her ass from pus filled papules. Quies literally had to submerge her ass in water with her panties still on to get them off. She assumed that she was having an allergic reaction to something she had bathed with only to take herself to Doctor's Care where they delivered the diagnosis of genital herpes. She shook her head as she slammed the door to her car. "Agghh!" she screamed in frustration while banging her head on the steering wheel repeatedly. "This is my pay back for having that abortion, I know it is." Quies cried continuing to feel sorry for herself.

Tap. Tap. Tap. Caught up in her emotions, Quies didn't notice the woman dressed in scrubs approach her car and knock on the window.

Quies rolled the window down. "Yes, can I help you with something?" she asked with tears streaking carelessly down her cheeks.

"Are you ok? I see that you're in distress. Do you require medical attention? If so, I can escort you inside the hospital and have you checked out," the nurse stated with concern etched on her face.

"No, ma'am. I'm fine. Just having a bad day," Quies informed while using the hem of her shirt to wipe snot and tears from her face.

The nurse smiled. "Prayer always helps, and I pray that whatever burdens your heart that God lightens you load. Give it to God, and he'll provide you with peace, sweetheart."

Tears fell from Quies's eyes again from the woman's kind words. She reached into the car, patted Quies on her shoulder and went about her business.

Quies inhaled and exhaled deeply, pulling what little strength she had out of her to press forward. *She's right, I do need to pray. I haven't done so in years.* "Lord please take this away from me. Everything and anyone who doesn't mean me any good, take them out of my life. Amen." She started her car and pulled out of the parking lot.

I got some'n for his ass. Since he wanna have other bitches at his spot, and I don't even know where the shit at. Fuck that, I'm goin' out and find me some new, clean dick. A man who knows how to treat a woman right is just what my heart needs.

Loose Lips...

"Girl, it is packed to the max out here tonight," Quies said slapping fives with Ebony.

"It's like this every Wednesday. I tried to tell you."

Ebony was a soldier in the army who had her hair styled by Quies. She was stationed in Fort Jackson. She's been in Columbia for a year now and met Quies through a friend, and they instantly clicked. Ebony was originally from Dallas, Texas, and loved the wild life when she wasn't in uniform. She was the spitting image of Paula Patton.

Ebony stepped out of her 2017 Audi A8, dressed in a black and grey Roberto Cavalli dress with Emporio Armani open toe heels on her small feet, looking like a movie star. Quies was dressed to the nines in a red, sleeveless, V-neck dress that fell just above her chunky thighs. The dress clung to her curves like plastic wrap with matching Prada peep toe heels with sexy ankle straps.

"Girl, I hope I can find a thugged out gentlemen in here, "Quies said.

"No, no, no, friend. We ain't doing the thugged out niggas tonight. They don't come with nothing but jumpsuits, bonds, and collect calls. Tonight, we on some grown man shit."

"I feel you, E, but ain't nothing like a thug, you hear me? That's all I know."

"Oh, trust me, a lot of these soldiers are with the shits. You'll find him girl. The men that frequent this spot have their shit together. All of them have careers. Step outside the box. A good man is out here, you just have to be open to it," Ebony offered giving Quies the game.

When they paid their fee and stepped into the club, it was much different from what Quies was used to. Of course, the thugs were in the midst, but you didn't see anyone snorting coke, popping pills, or smoking weed. She knew it was going to be a nice, casual night. One that didn't include drama. They got drinks and danced a little. So many guys approached them, but none received any play. That was until this one brother with neatly styled dreads, who stood about 6'2", 200lbs approached her, dressed casually in a pair of True Religion denim jeans, a green button down shirt, Black Nike boots, a platinum diamond pinky ring, and a nice watch.

"Excuse me, beautiful! I normally don't approach women in clubs, but your persona is attractive. My name is Brian," he provided, extending his hand.

Hypnotized by his hazel eyes that complimented his brown skin tone, she shook his hand without a second guess. She liked him instantly. He was clean and smelled good. She knew that he didn't smoke or partake in drugs because the whites of his eyes were clear.

"I'm Quies."

"Nice to meet you. I hope you don't mind me keeping you company for a few minutes. I'm here alone, and I see your friend is enjoying herself on the dance floor. I never saw you here! What brings you out tonight?"

"To be truthful, my so-called boyfriend isn't appreciative to have only me in his life, so I'm here to relieve some stress."

"Well, I 'm just on time to lend you a shoulder to lean on, free of charge."

They both laughed. Quies liked his personality, so they conversed over a little too many drinks. She was lit and enjoying herself so much, that she ended up leaving the club with him. They drove straight to a hotel and before the night was over, he knew who her boyfriend was, what he did for a living, and where he did it at, and he was all ears...

*****

Narcotics officers Steeples and his partner, Turner, also known as Rambo, rode through the city in Steeples' all black Charger with black 22-inch Voltron rims. Turner earned the name Rambo because he was built like him, looked like him, and he acted tough like him. They were talking about all the free money they've been making while listening to Young Jeezy's *Thug Motivation 101* album.

"Say, Brian, I've been your partner for over a year now, and I was wondering how you became so damn corrupt and mentally out of it."

"I never like talkin' about it, but if it will float yo' boat, I'll tell you," Brian replied.

"Hell, I've told you just about everything there is to know about me. I've had your back every step of the way. I figure that the least you can do is open up to me, unless you have something to hide," Rambo bluffed picking for information. They'd been playing Robin Hood for the past few weeks, robbing the dope boys and taking care of home with the funds and Rambo knew nothing about the man who had been assigned as his partner over six months ago.

"I don't have anything to hide, though I'm very private and to stick to myself. If you were my partner, you wouldn't be privy to anything I do, so, I'm gonna make it short because I hate talking about my past," Brian said.

Brian exhaled deeply before speaking. He stared off into the distance as if he were reliving what he were about to tell all over again. "I was ten years old when I learned that my father was strung out on drugs. He owed a drug dealer, robbed him or whatever the case was, but the dealer came to our home one night and shot up our house. My mom was hit in the chest and died instantly. My father hid out and I was taken into DSS custody before my paternal grandmother stepped in to raise me. I told myself that I would become a police officer when I got older and promised to make all drug dealers, thugs, and gang bangers suffer for the dirt they do. Plus, make them pay for my mother's death because her killer was never found. Then the situation that occurred last year only fueled my fire, and that is the reason somebody is about to give up some dope money or take a bullet, today!" Brian said, growing angry just talking about his past.

"Damn, B! I never knew it was like that. Now, I fully understand why you go so hard. I didn't know that your childhood had been so tough. I can only imagine what it's like to lose your mother at such a young age and your father to drugs. Damn," Rambo grunted feeling sorry for his comrade.

As they were talking, Brian was pulling into Ames Manor Projects. They eased up on a group of thugs who were posted by the mailbox. When they were close enough, Brian threw the car in park and they jumped out. Two of the guys ran before they could exit the car good. One attempted to pull his gun until he saw badges with guns pointed at his head. One ran too late and was run down by Brian. Brian clipped his feet and made him stumble forward, smacking his face on the pavement while losing a few teeth in the process. The blow left him dizzy, and by the time he was able to focus, Brian had him handcuffed walking back to his car.

"What the fuck you runnin' for, huh?" Brian asked as he roughly pushed the young thug against his car, smacking him upside the head hard in the process. "Spread yo' bony ass legs lil' nigga, before I break 'em!"

The young thug did as Brian demanded, even though he had no choice with Brian kicking the inside of his ankles to make sure his feet were spread. Brian patted him down and removed the money from his pockets and placed it in his own. Then he felt the front of the dude's crotch area.

"Come on, man. Why you playing all around a nigga's nuts?" the thug asked feeling violated.

"What you got in yo' pants, lil' nigga?" Brian turned the young buck around facing him. "Answer me, mufucka! What you got in yo' pants?"

The young man played stupid. Brian raised his knee in a karate move and kicked the jitty bug in the nuts with all his might buckling his knees. He collapsed to the ground in pain. Withering about the grass like a snake. Brian kneeled down over him. "When I ask you a question, you answer, bitch! Move yo' mufuckin hand."

The youngin' did as ordered while moaning and groaning in pain. Brian then slid his hand down dude's pants, coming out with about thirty dime bags of weed.

"Nigga, this all you got? Don't tell me you a petty ass weed man! I'ma have a smoke fest today with yo' life savings. Is that cool with you, playboy? Ol' nickel and diming ass nigga."

Brian tossed the bags to his partner who caught them midair.

"Man, that's all I mess with. Please don't take me to jail, man," he begged still cupping his sore nuts.

"Shut the fuck up and stop bitchin'. Ain't nobody gon' take yo' lil' punk ass to jail. Where yo' ID at?" Brian said as he searched the dude, not finding any identification. "What's yo' name, lil' nigga?"

"My name Vinson, man," he said.

"Well, Vint, I got some'n I need you to do for me, and maybe I won't lock you up, alright?" Brian said as he walked Vinson away from where Rambo had his friend.

"What's that, man?"

"I got some crack I want you to start sellin' for me."

"Man, I don't mess with that shit. Get me some weed, and I can shake that all day. I know nothing about coke."

"Well, nigga, you best learn. Watch a YouTube tutorial or something cause I want my goddamn money when I come through this bitch to pick it up. Check it. I'ma give you this crack pack, and you will get rid of it, or else you gonna go to jail after I shoot yo' soft ass. You got that?" Brian went back to his car and grabbed the bag of crack cookies from his trunk.

"This nine ounces. Give me at least $300 apiece. I know you can get $800 a pop for that pure, uncut shit. I'll come check on you in a week," Brian uncuffed him and handed him the dope. He refused to take it, so Brian pulled his gun, and shot Vinson in his right thigh. Vinson howled like a wolf while grabbing his thigh and collapsing to the ground.

He handed Vinson the work package again, but he was still reluctant to accept it.

"Take it, nigga, or the next one will leave you breathless," Brian threatened with the gun now pointed at Vinson's temple.

"This some bullshit, man," Vinson snatched the package from Brian's hand for fear that he would be shot again or probably killed. Blood oozed from Vinson's wound as he limped off in a hurry after receiving the bag of crack. This officer was on some *Training Day* shit and Vinson feared for his life. "Don't make me come back and murk yo' soft ass," Brian yelled.

Brian laughed while getting back in his car and waited for his partner to finish his business with the lil' dude he was harassing. He didn't give a fuck about Vint or the nosey ass neighbors because he was the law.

Rambo uncuffed the other dude, then hopped in the car and Brian pulled off.

"Check out this sweet 40 Glock the thug had. I might have to shoot his ass with it later because I took this from him," Rambo pulled a knot of money from his pocket and counted it.

"Here's half of it." He handed Brian $320.

"Okay. Count this right here," Brian said, as he handed Rambo a knot from his pocket. Rambo counted $223. He took a hundred dollar bill and handed the rest back to Brian. Brian stuffed the money back inside his pocket, then he pulled out the bag of weed from the same pocket. "Hand me a cigar from my glove box."

Brian pulled over at the Obama gas station on North Main. He rolled a blunt, lit it, and blew smoke from his nose. "Man, I don't see how you don't smoke any of this good shit right here," he said to Rambo, inhaling the weed smoke then pulling off into the North Main traffic.

"Smoking has never been my thing, but man, you's one crazy motherfucker, I love it," Rambo said.

Brian turned the volume up on Young Jeezy and headed down North Main Street. He pulled in the Gable Oaks Projects by building 25 and backed in so he could have a perfect view of the Bloods hanging by the park. He watched for a few minutes, then he decided the time was right to step from his car. Still smoking his blunt, looking like a thug from the streets, they walked towards a group of about twenty thugs, all dressed in red, male and female.

"Alright, y'all know what time it is!" Brian said as he took his last few pulls from his blunt.

The group of thugs started laughing and remained conversing with one another as if Brian and Rambo weren't even standing there. Brian thumped his blunt roach in the crowd, hitting one of the thugs arm. The thug turned around after looking at what it was that hit his arm. Then he puffed his own blunt a few more times and returned the gesture by thumping one right back at him, catching Brian in the chest.

"The fuck yo' problem is, homie?" he said as he reached for his burner, but Brian beat him at the draw. Then five more Bloods pulled out and pointed.

"Don't even think about it," Brian said, pulling his badge from inside his black t-shirt. Rambo followed suit. "Y'all punks, get on the ground."

"Fuck you, homie" one of the dudes said, and took off running. Brian quickly aimed his gun at the Blood and shot him in the ass.

Boom! One of them shot Brian, hitting him in the stomach, but it was blocked by his bullet proof vest.

The crowd of Bloods were all running in different directions shooting at the same time. *Boom! Boom! Boom! Boom!* Shots lit up the park every time a shot was fired. Bullets caused car alarms to go off as they ricocheted off the steel of playground equipment.

Boom! A bullet slammed into Rambo's back. He hollered as the metal pierced his skin but was protected by the bulletproof vest. He continued to chase the one who didn't have a weapon, catching and slamming him to the ground. Making him eat grass. Brian took cover behind a red 87' box Chevy with chrome rims. The firing ceased. After the quick shootout, Rambo and Brian robbed the dude they had and beat him bloody, then hopped in the charger and peeled out.

"Damn! That shit was wild. I always heard about how those Bloods in Gable Oaks got down, but I'll get back at them. We just gotta go at them stronger." Brian pulled over up the street on Colleton Street and asked Rambo to drive while he looked at his wound.

"Shit just find a spot to park. I took a hit my damn self and the shit feels like somebody is pouring alcohol mixed with salt in my wound. This shit hurts just as bad as actually being hit," Rambo informed while wincing in pain.

Brian pulled over, so they could examine their injuries. thankful that the vest had protected them. A true gunshot wound had to be reported and the last thing they needed was Internal Affairs breathing down their necks. They examined the points of entry to discover bruised, red areas on their skin. They both put their vest back on after plucking the bullets out. Brian rolled another spliff and instructed Rambo to drive to the Vista, so they could toss back some drink.

Teach A Man to Fish...

It was ten a.m. when Major woke up in Majesty's queen sized sleigh bed. He loved spending time with all three of his women, but he was truly in love with Majesty. She worked very hard to help make his phone store MajorWay Communication a success.

She knew about his other women but never complained or asked questions.

He was already fucking with Kimiko and Selah before they grew an attraction for one another. Truth be told, she was always too young, but now that she was twenty years old and a major part of his life, he kind of wished he was dealing with her before the other girls. But it was what it was. Majesty always played her position, and if she was involved with other niggas, she kept that shit quiet. He'd never gotten wind it. That's how respectful she was towards Major. He never saw anyone at her apartment, nor was she ever on the phone with other niggas. It was all about him. She was all for him and one day he would make her his wife. That was a fact.

Loyal women like Majesty were a rarity and hard to come by. She was a jewel that he intended to keep in his possession, but at the same time, all the women he dealt with were loyal in their own way.

His love for Kimiko remained stoic and at a standstill because she was infatuated with her child's father. For now, an enjoyment of friendship and digging in her guts from time to time would suffice, while it lasted. She was a good person who wanted to see him do well in life. He needed her positive energy and motivation in his life.

Kimiko was always educating him on other levels of getting money. She taught him about passive income and real estate. Things that would help in his transition from the streets.

Selah was his gangsta boo. She cooked coke, smoked with him, and moved weight. Whatever it took to keep money in Major's pocket, she was all for it. He loved that about her, but it also made her appear weak. He didn't want to deal with a woman who was more loyal to him than she was to herself. Selah could be bought and pimped, a deadly combination if her love was ever given to the wrong nigga, but he loved her still. Because she was Selah, raw and uncut.

Plus, that thug loving she provided was the truth. Yet, she had a lot of shit with her. She could be sneaky as fuck and hard headed at times.

Majesty was always about her business and a true friend who he could share anything with and not worry about hearing that shit in the streets later. A movement by herself, Majesty had the potential to be successful on her own. She didn't have her parents to back her up financially like Kimiko, but she gave Major investment ideas and preached to him about leaving the streets alone like Kimiko. Majesty had street and book knowledge. Everything about her was Grade A and on point.

As he lay in bed watching *Bangkok Dangerous*, Majesty bought him a tray filled with his favorite things to eat for breakfast. There was creamy grits, turkey sausage, scrambled eggs with cheese in them, and buttered toast, with a glass of orange juice and water to wash it all down with.

"I'll be in my office if you need me, babe. I'm about to get on the computer to do some research about a few things that will help you out in the streets."

"Like what?" he asked curiously.

"How to detect if yo' phone is tapped, ways to disguise your number when you call people without calling them from a private number, but if they call the number back on their caller ID, it won't be your actual contact number, how to disguise your voice with you speaking in your normal tone, how to send texts and make it appear as if it came from   somewhere else, and GPS tracking. Just ways to stop you from being indicted or caught up in any kind of way."

"Ok, G.I Jane. Now, you're really on some other shit!"

"Only because I love you, but please know this is only for you and yo' team. Everyone in the streets don't need to have this type of knowledge. This information in the wrong hands will have our asses facing football numbers," she said.

"It's this company called *Hacker 4 Hire,* and it teaches you all of that."

"Say no more, but what you think about moving out of here into a better spot because I don't like how Kisha be poppin' up and being all in our business? If you're with it, I want you under your own roof."

"I been ready to move. I just thought you needed me to be here because of the location. I'm close to everything right here."

"Hell nah. Find another spot, ASAP! Ion't care how much it costs either. Find something nice. A place I'll feel comfortable laying my head at night."

While they were talking, Major's phone vibrated on the nightstand on the side of the bed where Majesty stood. She grabbed his phone and threw it to him without looking at his caller ID. He answered, and it was Kimiko. Majesty overheard their conversation but continued about her business determined to stay out of his.

Two hours after making love to Majesty, Major pulled into the parking lot of Ruby Tuesday on Devine Street. It was Kimiko's lunch break and she wanted to talk with him about a few things. He hopped out of his trap mobile, which was a Toyota Camry with dark tint and walked into the restaurant to see his boo sitting in the back to his left at a table for two, sipping some water.

He had on a New Era Gamecock fitted cap, matching Gamecock crewneck sweat shirt,

 denim Levi's, and some Nike Air Max, looking like a true hustler. Kimiko loved his swag but wished he would tone that shit down and dress casual at times.

As he approached her, she stood up and greeted him with a hug and kiss, looking beautiful in her grey Viktor & Rolf pants suit and Casadei dress shoes.

"Hello, homey! How is your day, so far?" she asked as they sat down.

"What's up, boo? My day is lovely. What about yours? You smell edible by the way," he replied in his best proper voice, mocking her.

"Oh really? Everything's just peachy on my end. You know, just doin' what I love, teaching the kids how to read and comprehend."

The waitress came to their table. Kimiko had already ordered for the both of them. She ordered a rack of baby back beef ribs with a house salad for Major and a chef salad for herself. Then, he ordered a double shot of Grey Goose.

"Honey, what did I tell you about driving the hoopties? It's time you invest into a more presentable, luxury car or truck.

"I forgot that you're high maintenance, especially if you consider a Camry a hooptie. Those teachers at your job whip those. And, baby, I told you, I don't like looking too flashy, I ride low key.

"Major, those cars you drive, only say "hey, officer, stop me, I'm a drug dealer!" It's best to be in something conservative and dressed casually. That way, you look like an honest living, productive citizen, and not a thug. I love your swag, but you have to switch it up for certain occasions.

"I'll give it a try because what you're sayin' does make sense. I'll have the tints removed from the Camry."

"Thank you, honey," Kimiko said as she leaned over, politely touched his face, and kissed him on his cheek. "While we're on that subject. I want to ask you a question I was always curious about."

"What's that?"

"I was just wondering how you became the way you are. I mean, you're a good man with a humble heart, nice personality, but at the same time, there's this darkness to you." Major had to laugh at the way she expressed herself before giving her an answer.

"Well, baby, I grew up in the hood with my mom and dad. They used to drink heavily and use drugs. My mom has six kids, three boys, three girls, and no matter what, she never lost her temper with us. I guess that's where my patience and love comes from, but my dad is a gangsta. He robbed and killed, and in front of his kids if necessary. That's where the coldness originated. Growing up in the hood, you quickly become desensitized to shit that would unnerve others. My dad cheated on my mom, she grew tired of and that hood life and went to the rehab, got clean, found a good job as a nurse's assistant, and moved out of the hood into a better environment. I loved the hood, so I stayed with my dad and his other baby momma who lived in the same hood where I was raised. I loved being around the violence and dope dealers. My dad did his best raising me, but at a young age, I went out and got it how lived. I always was a hustla, but I had to learn how to balance having a good heart with having a cold heart because in the hood and anywhere in life, people will take advantage of you if you're weak, so I fought, stabbed, and shot people coming up. I learned to save money and protect it with my life. The more money and respect I gained, I became addicted to power. I'm a well-respected and connected young man."

"Well, just know that you can change your lifestyle now. You don't have to continue living the street life. You can further your education, take some vocational skills, get a legit hustle, and help the youth so they won't experience the same pain and struggles you did.

"All I know is the streets. What can I do legit?" he replied.

"Well, you can get into Real Estate and learn about investing in land and property. It just requires using your mind and communicating with people, which you are very good at. It's just like selling drugs, in a sense, except you're buying and selling houses and apartments, instead.

"You sound like you've been givin' this some thought, and I'm grateful for your concern and consideration. I'll give it a try because I don't want to be stuck in this lifestyle forever."

"Ok, I'm so happy for you, Major. That's what I love about you. You're thuggish and ghetto, but you're willing to use your potential and give yourself a chance to elevate and grow. Being willing is where it starts. Give a man a fish, and you feed him for a day. Teach a man to fish, and you feed him for a lifetime. I'll teach you everything I know about real estate, ok?" she told him.

Kimiko also earned a sizeable income from buying and selling houses. Both her parents are Real Estate Brokers who schooled her on the importance of having multiple streams of income. She grew up knowing the business, and now Major was about to learn all that she did.

"Thank you, Miko. I'm always up for learning new things, especially if it involves keeping some money in my pocket and building a legacy. The best thing someone can give you is the opportunity to take care of yourself." Major ordered another double shot of Goose and held it up to Kimiko's glass of water. "To health, wealth, and happiness."

They toasted, then threw their drinks back. Kimiko had just gotten a few brownie points for that one because Major was ready to do something with his life and stop being in the streets so much.

"Determination, ambition, drive, and motivation is all you need, baby. I 'm about to show you how to really get paid," she said. "I guess it's time I get back to work."

Kimiko paid for their orders with her credit card, and Major left a ten dollar tip. Then, they went to their cars, which were parked next to each other. He gave her a passionate hug and kiss.

"Thank you, Kimiko."

"For what, honey?"

"For caring and believing in me."

I Ain't Taking No Losses...

Major and Fresh sat in Trina's den smoking Purple Thrax trying to figure out what was going on in the city with the dirty police robbing their workers. Since Fresh and Trina got out of the hospital, they've been spending a lot of time together. Fresh felt bad that she was shot behind his mess. He was more impressed that she didn't tell the investigator anything about his lifestyle because they were really concerned about how he made his living. Also, he didn't like how Quies was running the streets lately and ignoring his calls, so he took all his clothes from her house and moved in with Trina until he got another spot.

"Man, I've lost over forty grand from them dirty ass narcos, not counting the soldiers who got locked up," Major said. "From payin' niggas' bonds and lawyer fees, I'm hustling backwards as fuck."

"You ain't the only one, bruh. I'm takin' big losses, and you know my good splurgin' ass can't afford that," Fresh complained.

"They hit my lil' cousin' in the Colonies, too," Trina said, as she walked in the den to grab a cigar from her glass table.

Major looked up at her wondering why she was all in their business. Fresh caught the side eyed look Major shot in Trina's direction. *I swear this nigga keep an ignorant, nosey ass bitch around.*

"Spread ya' hustle, baby. This grown man bitness. Go paint yo' toenails or something, but get the fuck outta our face," Trina sucked her teeth before stomping off down the hallway.

They resumed conversing once she was out of listening range.

"We gotta find a way to bump into these mufuckas because they fuckin' with the wrong nigga shit, and that fuckin' K-9 they using, I got some'n for his ass. Watch what I tell ya," Major said, angrily.

"Them mufuckas extortin' them boys and all. The only reason I ain't post up and wait on them yet is because I'm still healin', but when I do, I'll be at one of my traps waitin' on them niggas. I'm opening mufuckas up, no questions asked. I ain't taking no loses. I got heat, baby!"

"Shid, they tried hittin' Gable Oaks, but Wayko and his goons aired they asses out. They say everybody talkin' bout that black Charger wit the stick up narcos. Man, you need to heal up, so we can see bout these niggas fuckin' up our paper. We need all our solid soldiers if we going against crooked cops. Those niggas operate on a whole 'nother level."

"Nigga, if you need me to, we can get on that shit now. I ain't fuckin' handicap, just a lil' slow. I still can pop them cannons," Fresh replied.

"Nah, bruh. While you healin', it'll give me time to put a good, reliable plan together. We can't move sloppy," Major said, as he grabbed his phone from his hip.

"Hello! Yeah... yeah, we can do that. Alright, see you then."

"Sound like a meat mission," Fresh joked, always having his mind on the pussy.

"That was Kimiko. I'm bout to haul ass, bruh. I got a dinner date," Major said as he got up to leave.

Suddenly, walking in the den was Trina's friend, Tip. "Nigga, you need to give me some more of that dick while you treatin' bitches to dinner and shit," she said.
"Real women don't allow others to fix their man's plate. All you gotta do is come to my house, and I'll be more than happy to feed yo' sexy, red ass."

"Trina!" Major yelled. "Come get yo' company, all in my fuckin' business. If you wasn't so damn controlling, a nigga would come through and drop some dick off in you once in a while, but you don't respect a nigga's level. Need to sit yo' ass down somewhere with that aggressive shit. Women don't holla at me; I holla at women. Y'all hoes kill me shootin' y'all shot at a nigga. Don't. Following up with social media got y'all looking stupid and desperate as fuck. Now move outta my way!" Major chastised, shoving her hot pussy ass to the side.

"Whatever! I hope ya' dick fall off." she said.

Major shook his head. "Won't fall off in yo' ass. You must got some shit you tryna give away, you so anxious for a nigga to tap it," he shot back at her with a wink.

"Bruh, I'm out."

School had just let out. Kimiko was still in her classroom grading students' quizzes. She didn't have to pick BJ up from daycare until six pm, so she decided to do something constructive with her time. Life was good, and her mind was clear. She had a date with her boo later and couldn't wait to see him. As she graded papers and anticipated her night, she just knew nothing could frazzle her peaceful, jolly mood, until she heard her classroom door open and looked up. With a disgusted look on her gorgeous face, "what're you doing here?" she questioned. "I have work to do, if you don't mind."

"Can't a man visit the love of his life?" he said.

"Brian, I'm over you. I have a new love in my life, and I'm more than happy watching it grow. "

He walked up behind her as she remained seated. He swiftly grabbed her by her ponytail then whispered "I miss you" against her ear. She tempted to pull away, but his grip only became firmer, tighter.

"Uhh! Brian, you're hurting me," she moaned in pain.

"Just like you're doin' me. How do you think I feel not being able to see and love you like we used to, huh?" he said as he yanked her hair, causing it to frizz.

"Brian, you chose to stop coming around. I moved on. I can't allow you to come in and out of our lives. You don't spend time with me or our son. I've moved on, and if you want to work out visitation for BJ, cool, but I'm over you, and I'm over us, Brian. "

"No, it's not over, Kimiko, until I say so! You hear me?" he said, suddenly biting her in the face, leaving deep teeth marks.

"Oooouuuucchh! Brian, what is wrong with you?" she yelled, touching her face, looking at the small specks of blood on her hand.

Her scream alerted a few teachers who rushed into her classroom to make sure she was alright.

"What is going on in here, Kimiko?" an elder lady asked.

"Mrs. Carson, this is BJ's father. He has lost his mind and I want him to leave these premises," Kimiko said, feeling a lot safer having the teachers around. With witnesses present, Brian wouldn't harm her further.

"Kimiko, you are bleeding! Did he hit you?" another teacher asked with a hand covering her mouth in surprise.

"No, Mrs. Faulkner, he bit me!"

"I'm calling the police, right now!" Mrs. Carson said, as she turned to leave Kimiko 's classroom.

"That won't be necessary. I am the police. I can escort myself out, but you'll be seeing me again soon, very soon," Brian said as he left the building. His words caused a shiver to travel down her spine. She had never witnessed that look in his eyes. He was bordering insanity, and Kimiko didn't know what to do next.

"Kimiko, we won't tolerate that kind of behavior in this school. You can't work around the children with bruises on your face," Mrs. Faulkner stated.

"I know, and I apologize. It won't happen again. Can we please keep this between us three?" Kimiko begged looking from one teacher to the next.

"I need this job."

"Kimiko, you can't apologize for his stupidity. If he would do it once, he'll do it again. You need to have him arrested for his abuse, immediately."

"I'm afraid, Mrs. Carson. He's an officer himself, and they stick together more than you'll ever know. They follow a creed that we civilians will never understand."

Mrs. Carson shook her head in dismay. Kimiko was making excuses for him. *If she really wanted to press charges, she'd do so. Cameras are in every hallway and classroom throughout the school. All she'd have to do was show a judge camera footage to get a restraining order*, but this wasn't her battle to fight, so she kept her thoughts to herself.

"It's your life, child. Don't let this linger. Get help while you can because you may not have another chance to have him arrested if he catches you somewhere and can't control his anger. You were lucky this time. If you need me, I'm here for you," Mrs. Faulkner, another teacher present spoke up and said.

"Thank you, guys, but I'll be alright."

*****

"Major, are you okay? Majesty asked.

"Yeah, I'm good," he replied. But Majesty knew better. She knew his temperament and studied his mood. Something was bothering him.

"You look worried, baby."

"I was supposed to get wit Kimiko, but she ain't call me yet. That's not like her to not be punctual for a date." He was all in his feelings.

"Maybe something more important came up. A family emergency. Just pray that she's alright and not think the worst all the time. I'm sure it couldn't be helped and that she has a logical explanation for standing you up," Majesty said, trying to keep him thinking positively.

"Yeah, you right," he agreed, but deep down he couldn't help but think that maybe she was with her baby daddy. He decided to call and got no answer, so he got undressed and relaxed on Majesty's couch and rolled a blunt.

Majesty saw the hurt in his expression. She positioned his body between her legs and massaged his neck and back.

"Baby don't let it frustrate you. You have to stay in control of your emotions because situations occur that you have no control over. You have to learn to accept the things you can't change and deal with them accordingly in a positive manner. Be patient. You'll find out the reason for her absence."

Major relaxed a little after her encouraging words. That's why he loved her so much. She never asked personal questions, she just comforted him and gave the best advice. As he relaxed in her lap, thinking about what she was saying, he eventually dozed off.

A few hours later, he was awaken by Majesty blessing him with some of the best slow head a man could ever want.

Majesty held his meat in a vice grip as she spit on the crest before suctioning him deeply into her mouth. His Johnson tickled her tonsils.

"Damn baby, that shit feel good as fuck," he groaned humping her mouth.
Majesty's oral assault had his toes balled into a fist.

She spit on his stick again. Soaking his joystick while working her hands in a ring motion. Major placed his hands on Majesty's ears and bounced her head in his lap.

Majesty teased his meat, deep throating his sausage until her nose touched his stomach, then withdrawing and licking the crest. Major's eyes rolled into the back of his head.

"No, baby. Look at me. Watch me milk this dick," she mouthed.

Major opened his eyes to see Majesty staring seductively back at him. She had a mouth full of big dick, and to see it in her oral grip caused all the blood to rush to the tip of his meat.

Her mouth was so warm and caressing.

Hmmm, humm, hummm she hummed on his soul pole. The sensation causing his seed to boil within his scrotum. She was giving him that toe curling necktarine. He was in a zone, humping her mouth, waiting to catch his nut. Majesty applied more suction, using her index and thumb to create an O around his dick as she sucked. The motion sent him over the edge, and within seconds, his seeds were washing down her throat. Majesty swallowed every drop of his stress juice.

"Damn, baby, you really know how to make a nigga feel like the man."

"I aim to please, baby. Whatever makes you happy is what I intend to do." She got up from her knees, wiping her mouth with the back of her hand before disappearing into the restroom and brushing her teeth thoroughly, then sat at her computer.

He zipped his pants and walked up and stood behind her to see what she was up to.
"Baby, you know they closed down Club Bikini," she said. "I was thinking that you should grab the building and re-open it with a new name."

"You think so?"

"Yeah, I know so. The boy Vereen is in jail. He opened the club with money made from a fraudulent federal income tax scheme. He was indicted by the feds, and now his spot is up for grabs."

"Say no more, I'm with it if you think it's a good move. Do whatever you have to do to make it happen."

"I know it's a good move. It's in a prime location, close to everything. The city needs a hot night spot for people to link up at. Your go head was all the confirmation I needed," she responded excitedly.

*****

Setting out some new phones in her store on Sparkleberry Lane, Majesty noticed a couple in the Wendy's parking lot having a physical altercation, so she went outside and sat in her car to be nosey. The female tried holding her own until dude gave her a powerful smack. When the female tried to run, that's when Majesty was able to see her face.

Her mouth fell into an "O" as the altercation unfolded before her. She couldn't believe what she was seeing. *That's why she probably stood Major up. She got a man, one that whoops her ass in public too.* Majesty said to herself. Majesty didn't know whether to call the police or help her. "Nah, fuck that. I'ma sit my ass right here. Those licks ain't meant for me," she decided to stay out of it and mind her business, because, obviously, they knew each other really well.

"He oughta be ashamed of himself putting his hands on that little ass woman. Bet he won't run up on Major like that, bitch ass."

Majesty pulled out her phone to record the rest of the commotion. She rolled down her window to hear what was being said but dialog was muffled due to nearby traffic. A small crowd had started to form. Eventually, someone was able to pull the man off Kimiko's ass. She was crying, and her face was bright red. Tears and snot covered her face. Majesty felt sorry for her. Even with the man holding him off Kimiko's ass, he was still trying to break free to attack her some more.

Several guys tried attacking Kimiko's abuser, but he pulled a gun. "Y'all mufuckas betta back up!" he yelled before pulling his weapon from behind his back.

"Oh, shit," Majesty exited her car as her eyes landed on the shiny black firearm. That was her cue to get the hell out of dodge. She half ran, half walked to get back into the safety of the store.

From the windows, she could see the small crowd disperse. People were tripping over their feet and seeking cover behind parked cars.

The man then hopped into his car burning rubber as he sped away.

Majesty called Major. "Baby, you're not gonna believe what I just saw. Kimiko was just getting her head rocked by some nigga in the Wendy's parking lot. I got video too. Check your email. I'm about to send it to you."

*****

Major's blood ran hot after viewing the video of the man beating on Kimiko. Any man who can put his hands on a female was a coward in his book. He dialed Kimiko's number. After several rings she finally answered.

"I see you got niggas speed bagging your head, now."

"Well, hello to you too Andre? What are you talking about?" she deflected, trying to throw him off by calling him by his government.

"I'm talkin' 'bout the nigga that was beatin' yo' ass today in the Wendy's parking lot."

"Huh? That wasn't me! I don't know what you're talking about. Why would you ask me a thing like that?" she lied raking her brain trying to figure out how he knew about what transpired.

Major let out an exasperated sigh, "damn, you lying to a nigga now? I'll holla at you later though, Kimiko. Have a good evening, enjoy," he uttered before disconnecting the call.

This Our City...

Major was at Majesty's house filling two vacuum cleaners with cash when he received a call from his little brother, Taliban, telling him how two narcos came to the hood on some "lay down" bullshit and they shot it out.

"Stop bullshittin', bruh!" Major said.

"Nigga, Lump is in the hospital having bullets removed as we speak! I shot the black one with the dreads in the stomach, then we got light."

"Alright, Ban. Y'all lay low, and I'll fuck with you later. Aye, bruh, what were they ridin' in?"

"A black on black Charger, and, bruh, the nigga walked up on us smokin a fuckin' blunt. Them mufuckas wildin' dawg, for real."

"I hear ya'. Keep yo' phone on, I'll holla back later."

Major called for a meeting with his brothers and a few of his workers from different projects to discuss how they should handle the crooked narcos. They all met up in Willow Lakes apartments. It was over a hundred people out there: some Bloods, Crips, Folk, Gangster Disciples, and regular hustlers and gangsters who didn't bang. Under Major's tutelage, they all stood united for one common cause: to get money, and murder if necessary, but all of them are on Major's team.

"I'm sho' we've all heard or experienced the two narcos that are robbing our spots. I've had five of my personal trap houses hit, and Fresh had at least seven of his hit. Of course, some bucked the jack and went to jail, costing us a lot of unnecessary money paying bonds and lawyers' fees, on top of losing dope and money. We have no way of knowing who they are right now, but I suggest that we all continue to get money. For the ones who drop off and leave, we will resume posting up again and participate in finding these crabs. We need to be so deep that they won't think about trying no stupid shit. Some of us can post outside to draw them in and others can lay low inside, so they will think our soldiers are alone, but when they try to hit, we all pop up on their asses with the element of surprise, busting! Point. Blank. Period."

"Hell, yeah! That's what the fuck I'm talm 'bout!" one dude yelled.

"Damn right!" belted another. Major raised his hand to regain control of the crowd.

"One band, one sound. We all operate on one accord. From this point forward, we ain't letting the police raid us or get close enough to even search any of us. All that shit is dead. They exit their cars, we shoot, fuck'em. They want g-shit, so we gonna give it to them raw. It's time we let them know we run these streets. Fuck the law. If you ain't with it, find another city to hustle in because if yo' name comes up for not ridin' for the home team, you die. Straight like that! This meeting is adjourned," Major said as he walked behind one of the buildings and hopped the brick wall where he used to post in Willow Runs Projects and headed to check on Mook. Mook had been hiding out from Major for about a month now; he owed him twenty grand for a kilo. Mook wasn't home, so Major walked back to post up with Von and his boys who hustled for him. He knew Mook was dodging him but decided to let it be and handle it when the time came.

Major walked up on Von dressed in his get money, kill a nigga gear. Niggas thought he had gotten too big time to hang, but Major was a street nigga at heart. Nothing or no one would keep him from his hood. He just felt that it was a time when you had to pull up, and a time to fall back. Once you elevated in the game it was customary to relocate because of status, but he was on a mission and fully prepared.

Major, Fresh, and Von posted and kicked shit like they came up doing, except for now, Von operated the hood. Major left him in charge and was more than impressed by the way Von handled his business. All his workers were on point and serious about their business. Von handled the block better than Major did, and that's the reason he left him in charge and not Fresh. Von proved that he was capable of handling that position ever since he witnessed Major front Mook that ounce.

"Nigga, I see you out here handling yo' business, " Major complimented.

"I learned from the best," Von replied.

"Shit, I'ma ask you for a job in bout a year, the way you got traffic comin' through this bitch. I even see a few of my old serves coppin' from you, my nigga."

"Nigga, you can have them back, but I capitalized from yo' flaws. Don't hate, congratulate."

"I ain't mad at ya'. You got shit on lock. I'm just glad that we on the same team."

After a few hours of posting up, Von had easily made over thirty grand. They decided to go in Selah's apartment so Von could count his earnings. Von sold damn near half a brick in ounces. Milking the game off pieces. After about an hour of counting money and smoking blunts, Von's Nextel chirp began to go off and he walked off, leaving Major and Fresh standing in the kitchen talking shit. Before Von could say hello, a thunderous bang could be heard before the door flew off its hinges and smacked against the wall. Three masked men came running in one behind the other.

"Get down! Get down, now! Where's the money and dope at?" one of them yelled as they each went around slamming the women to the floor. The women were in hysterics screaming and crying loudly. "Shut the fuck up!" one of them ordered causing the house to fall silent. The only noise that could be heard was chirping from Von's phone.

Major and Fresh heard the commotion; they thought it was the police kicking in the door. With his adrenaline pulsing, he realized that he didn't hear anyone yelling police.
That was his cue to let his cannon bust.

He peeked his head around the kitchen wall and saw the men standing over the women and Von with weapons drawn.

"It's a jack," Fresh whispered with his hammer cocked. Major let his .44 bulldog bark shooting from the kitchen, which caught the masked men completely off guard.
Boom! Boom! Boom! The first shot slammed into his target's face, exploding his head like a watermelon hitting the pavement. Brain matter splashed against the wall before his body hit the floor landing next to Triece. The second shot ripped through the sheetrock on the walls, but that third shot caught another man in the neck. Blood squirted from its point of entry. He staggered out

the door behind his comrade firing wildly before making his exit. Fresh and Major came from their post letting off round after round.

Shots could be heard popping off outside, alerting them that their team was handling business. Fresh stepped over the dead man and a pool of blood that had begun to circle around his head. He looked out into the stairwell to ensure that the enemy was gone. Seeing no sign of them, he attempted to secure the door.

"Fuck!" Von yelled, still in shock standing from his prone position on the floor.

"It's all good. Shit was self-defense. Is everybody aight?" Major asked the women who were still crying. Von and Selah's mom pulled herself up and started rocking while still seated on the floor.

Von went over to his mother, squatting before her. "It's aight, mama. You straight." She continued to cry on his shoulder as he tried to console her.

"Triece, Quies, y'all good?" Fresh asked.

"I'm straight," Triece concurred, pulling herself up and going over to Von. She threw her arms around his neck before kissing his face. "Damn, that scared the hell outta me, baby. What we gonna do about this body, y'all?"

Quies was in a state of shock and bleeding from her right shoulder.

"Oh shit, man! Quies caught a hot one. Quies hit! " Von said.

Fresh and Major walked over to her. "She'll be alright, " Major said as he pulled back her t-shirt a little. "It only grazed her shoulder. It's gonna bleed like crazy, but she ain't gotta go to the hospital."

"Snap out of it, baby. You good. Lemme see. Aye, Selah, go get something so we can bandage this shit up." Fresh asked. When Quies heard that she only had a flesh wound, she snapped out of her reverie. She looked at her shoulder. "Shit, I thought I was a goner."

"It's only a paper cut, baby." Fresh added as he applied pressure on her shoulder to stop the bleeding. As the women got up from the floor and checked on Quies's wound, the distinctive sirens of the ambulance and fire trucks could be heard off in the distance.

Von handed Triece the money he had on him. "Go put this up, baby." If he was going to jail, he didn't want to have any money on him.

Triece left to do as asked and came right back.

When the ambulance finally arrived to their apartment, they were all curious to know how the paramedics knew they needed assistance.

No one in the dwelling had used the phone. Something wasn't right, and all of them sensed it. When the police officers stepped inside the apartment, they didn't speak, neither did they inquire regarding what transpired. They ordered everyone to sit on the living room sofa. "Hands on your knees where we can see them!" one of the deputies ordered.

The group did as asked, but their body language revealed their frustrations.

"Why y'all treating us like we're guilty? This my mama house, and those niggas kicked the door in," Selah informed with sass.

"Damn right. This shit right here is self-defense," Von added pointing at the deceased.

The deputies continued to ignore them. "Remove the mask. Let's see what we have here?"

The other attending officer went over to remove the mask, nearly busting his ass in the thick puddle of blood that circled the dead man's body. The officer pulled the ski mask up and over his head revealing a face no one in the room had seen before, but the look on the deputy's face spoke volumes. Von, Major, and Fresh exchanged glances.

"That nigga, twelve. I can tell from the looks on they faces," Fresh mouthed.

The officer had a nasty look on his face once he stood up. With his upper lip curled, he spoke through clenched teeth, "who did the shooting?"

"I did. They came in here with choppas pointed and ordered everyone to lay down. I shot him in self-defense!" Major exclaimed, taking full responsibility for his actions. He assumed that what he did was justified, but he was wrong.

"Stand up and place your hands behind your back," the officer ordered with his hand on his weapon.

"For what?" everybody asked.

Major did as told. "Place my hands behind my back for what? I didn't do shit wrong."

"For the murder of Officer Turner," he informed while handcuffing Major and reading Miranda Rights.

"Hell no! That mufucka and his goons broke in our apartment and tried to rob us. Y'all ain't chargin' me for no fuckin' murder. This shit is illegal because his fuckin' partners ran off and left this man. Selah call my lawyer."

"Ok, baby. I'm calling right now!" Selah said with tears streaking down her face.

Major was arrested and charged with a capital felony for the murder of a law enforcement officer and transported to Alvin S. Glenn Detention Center.⏹

Play If You Want To...

Von was holding things down in Major's absence. Major was being held with no bond. It had been a month since he'd been gone, and the streets weren't the same without him. Even though he was gone, he still got shit done from behind bars. His crew still needed to eat, and money was to be made. Von had just over a hundred thousand dollars of Major's money. Funds he'd use to keep operations afloat. The streets needed work, so Major had his people deliver product to Von.

Von had his boy, Bub helping him make moves. He and Bub played with the green plastic army men as kids and ate free lunch together in Latimore Manor. Bub always played fair, and Von was glad he had him by his side. "Aye, Bub, I need you to take two ounces over to Fam in Meadow Lakes," Von said.

"I can handle that. You got it ready?"

"Just need to bag it up. Hold on," Von paused the PlayStation three, grabbed the scale and the coke sitting on the glass table in front of him, and weighed the two ounces in two separate sandwich bags. The cocaine was all solid powder, except for maybe five grams in each bag.

He handed it to Bub, and Bub was out the door to handle business.

Bub hit the automatic start from his keychain to Von's two door SS Monte Carlo. He backed out and drove straight to Flying J's gas station. Inside the store, he grabbed a few packs of coffee creamer and Newports. He got back in the car, took out five grams of coke and replaced it with five grams of creamer. He dipped his pinky nail in his personal bag, then headed to Meadow Lakes. Fam had people waiting on him, so he didn't waste time cooking his work once it got in his hands, but it wasn't bouncing back like it was supposed to do. "This some straight bullshit. Let me call this nigga," he mumbled.

"Yoo, what up, fam?" Von said.

Fam placed the call on speaker as he continued to manipulate the product. "Don't know what's goin' on, but every time you send old girl by ya' boy Bub, she always seem to be acting funny with me. I don't know if she got his nose wide open or what, but, bruh, you need to come scoop this bitch up," Fam explained regarding the coke in code.

"Bruh, it gotta be a misunderstanding. Ole girl my bitch, and I know my dawg wouldn't fuck with her behind my back," Von said.

"Come holla at me and see what's on her mind then. She actin' stubborn as hell, bruh. You know I wouldn't come at you sideways."

"Alright, I'll be at you shortly, bruh. "

Von didn't tell Bub where he was headed. He just grabbed the keys to the trap mobile, hauling ass to meet Fam. Fam was a solid, good nigga whose word was bond. He went to check out the problem. He pulled up, got out the car, and waited for Fam to come to the gate to get his crazy ass pit bull.

When they stepped in the kitchen, Von noticed how the work was clung to the glass. A clear indication that the work had been stepped on more than sidewalks. "I don't believe this shit! Bub must've put flour or some'n in this shit."

Von reached inside his pocket. "Here, bruh. I bought two more with me just in case. I apologize for his fuck up. I had a few other people complain, but I ain't want to believe it. Plus, one of my bitches told me he be hangin' with her coke snortin' ass brother. You callin' with a complaint ain't shit but confirmation that the nigga getting his nose dirty. I'ma handle it, bruh, and from now on, we deal directly." Von said.

Before Von left, he put some more water and soda in the jars and brought the work back to life. He knew what to do because niggas used to do him the same way, so it all comes from experience. "Goddamn, nigga, you a certified chemist," Fam complimented after witnessing Von bring the work back from death.

"Comes from experience. It's nothing. Keep all that shit. Gotta right that nigga wrong, you feel me?"

Von and Fam dapped up. Von headed back to the hood to holler at Bub. *It's back to hugging the block with his slick ass. Nigga can't be trusted. Try to elevate his ass and he levitating by getting high off the product. Niggas!*

*****

Fresh sat in Trina's living room sipping on the last drop of Grey Goose. He thought about calling Trina and telling her to bring him another bottle on the way home but thought better of it. He needed to fall back off that bottle. Lately, he'd been losing money or miscalculating it.

Drinking daily and partying all week had just about leveled his pockets. From his reflection in the mirror, he'd also picked up a little weight. "Damn a nigga done let his self-go. Shid, at least I'm eating good." His midsection sat atop his man meat. He had that Gucci Mane physique before he went to do fed time. Major had left Fresh five kilos before his unfortunate incarceration. Fresh sold four of them, but barely had enough money to pay for three kilos. He'd been splurging like crazy and buying a little pussy here and there, but not that damn much. "I know good and goddamn well I ain't paid for that much pussy. Something ain't right. I swear fo' God, I think I gotta hole cut in all my pants pockets," he said aloud, polishing off the rest of his drink before belching loudly and hitting his chest.

The numbers weren't adding up and he had nothing to show for his efforts. He surmised that he may have given someone work on consignment or misplaced a kilo.

"That's bullshit though." He reasoned the liquor was thinking for him. He knew better. Dope boys didn't misplace kilos.

"I gotta stop drinking and ballin' and get back on my grind. I need to find somebody to cop a few bricks from so I can make sho' Major shit is paid for," Fresh thought.

"Fuck it! That nigga ain't getting outta jail, anyway."

Fresh told himself that he was going to sleep the hangover off. Tomorrow he would rise and grind. Right now, he was hustling backwards. He'd only been asleep for a few hours when cold steel slamming across his face awoke him from his stupor.

Boom! Boom! Major fired two shots next to Fresh's head that ruptured his eardrum. He snapped out of his liquor induced coma, grabbing his ear and pulled back a hand filled with blood.

"What the fuck, bruh? This is me!" he screamed now hard of hearing.

"Nigga, fuck you! Get yo' pussy ass up. You thought I wasn't getting outta jail, huh, nigga?" Major gritted with a snarl before slapping Fresh again across the face with his .44 Bulldog.

"Oh, you think it's a game? Niggas told me how you been in the clubs makin' it rain with my fuckin' money, but you too busy to come and see ya' dawg? Couldn't even drop a nigga a kite or send commissary money? Well, I'm back, my nigga. Now, let's get yo' drunken ass up and get my fuckin' money."

Major grabbed Fresh by his Polo shirt, pushing him towards the back bedroom. The room began to rotate. It felt as if someone had placed him in a washing machine. Everything was spinning.

"Aight, Major, man! Damn! Calm the fuck down! This me, ya' dawg! I got you, man. You know I ain't never played you about no bitness, bruh," Fresh pleaded, as he went to Trina's closet and pulled out a safe.

"Bruh" my ass, nigga. Just run me my money or Mrs. Drake gon' be standing ova yo' bitch ass cryin!"

Fresh opened the safe, grabbed the four stacks of money, and tried to hand it to Major.

Major eyeballed the money and knew Fresh was short. "How much money is that, Fresh?"

This is sixty grand, bruh, and I still got this brick." *Wham!* Major smacked Fresh across the face with the gun. Fresh hollered as blood flew from his nose and mouth. A huge gash opened down the center of his forehead where the bridge of his nose meet his eyes.

"Nigga, where the rest of the dope and money at? I ain't gon' ask yo' ass no mo'!"

"Bruh, I fucked up! I'll rob every dope boy in the city and pay you back, bruh. Just give me a few days, bruh, I swear," Fresh pleaded.

"Fuck that shit you talkin'. You had two whole months to get right, nigga! It's too late for all that. Now you die!" Major lifted his .44 aiming it at Fresh's forehead, about to squeeze the trigger. All Fresh did was close his eyes and whisper a prayer of forgiveness, hoping Major would give him a chance to repay him. The thunderous bark of the bulldog ended that hope...

"Fresh! Fresh!" a female voice said.

"No, Major! I'm sorry, bruh! Pleeaase!" Fresh begged tossing, kicking, and throwing punches in his sleep. *Splash!*

Trina doused him with a pot of water. He jumped up off the sofa breathing heavily as if he were about to drown in a pool.

"Girl, what the fuck!?"

"Nigga, you was having a nightmare. What you did to be Major that got you beggin' and apologizing in yo' sleep? Yo' ass need to stop drinkin', boy!" Trina said, shaking her head in pity while picking up the empty Grey Goose bottle and throwing it away.

Fresh placed his hand to his ear then withdrew his palm. "No blood. I can hear!" The dream he had was so vivid that he had a hard time processing that he was awake, alive and well.

Trina shook her head, "and why would you not be able to hear? On God, you need to leave that damn drink alone. You can't handle that shit."

"You right, boo! I been dreamin' some crazy ass shit. I pray that shit don't eva come true. For real, for real," Fresh said, then he looked at the clock on the cable box.

"Damn! I been sleep for four hours. I got to get my ass to the hood," he said. He got up, went to his safe, and weighed a half of key. He had a quarter kilo left and was going to get every dime out of the remaining work, cop a few bricks, and get that money back straight before Major came home. That nigga was known for clawing his way out of sticky situations, and when he touched down, Fresh would have every dime of his money.

Outta Sight, Outta Mind...

Major was mentally exhausted from thinking about his situation and how fucked up it was. He thought about calling his contact and have her pull some strings but decided to leave it in God's hands. He hadn't heard a word from any of his so-called friends and family who claimed to love him. Other than Von, his mom, his oldest sister, Sonya, his cousin, Kim, and of course, Majesty. Those were the people who were always available when he called or needed them.

Even Fresh was treating him like a stranger. *As long as he got my paper when I bounce, we'll be alright.* Major thought to himself. He didn't know what Selah's problem was, but he knew her kind, so he ain't let it worry him. Outta sight, outta mind.

Major could pretty much guess what Kimiko was doing. "Probably running behind her baby daddy who beats her ass," he huffed.

Kimiko was nothing but a spoiled ass rich girl. Females like her always needed attention. It was just in their character.

He decided to call a few people, so he waited in line for a phone to become available. When one finally did, he tried calling Selah again, but got no answer. He also tried Kimiko again but received no response from her either.

He cursed under his breath so none of the other inmates would know that he was in his feelings. It bothered him how the people he valued most and held in high regard had completely turned their backs on him. It was like he had already been found guilty, the way his loved ones were condemning him.

When I get outta here, I'ma give all them bastards my ass to kiss. Major was too good of a dude for people to play him to the left. Inwardly, he promised that this would be the last time they caught him in a vulnerable position like this. With his emotions running high and his spirits dampened, he called the person who was always there, no matter what. *I swear when I exit this bitch, I'ma make Majesty a priority instead of my last resort.*

"What's up, sexy?" Majesty answered.

The melody of her voice was music to his ears. The sweet tenor caused his heart to swell and a smile to cross his lips. "Ain't too much, just wanted to make sho' you were good."

"Yeah, you know me. I'm just makin' sure the businesses are performing to the best of their abilities. The club is blowin' up. Yo' boy Cedric is a good business partner. I've gotten really close to his wife, LaShon."

"That's good. I knew it would be a perfect fit," Major said.

"The Love-Nest is a money magnet. We have all the strippers buying up the porn videos and sex toys. I have to say that you know what brings in the money."

"That's what it's all about, capitalizing and being comfortable. But check this out, I want you to send my Real Estate books, I need to study that material while I have free time on my hands."

Ok, I'll do that when we hang up, but are you ok? Do you need a visit or anything? You sound defeated. Are you giving up on yourself?" Majesty inquired picking up on his lackluster spirit."

"Nah, I'm good. I won't lie and say that sitting idle ain't fuckin with me, but I'll be aight. I just need those books. They'll put my focus on other shit. Ya' know? I need to get my mind right before I get outta here. I'm gon' become a successful business man. These crackers talkin' bout givin' me the death penalty but watch how I wiggle outta this shit and still have a sane mind frame."

"I know you'll be ok. Just stay in your Bible, ok? I love and miss you, Major. Keep your head up and your spirits high baby."

When they hung up the phone, Major decided to see what the news was talking about. WachFox57 was just coming on.

"Columbia police are investigating the shooting death of a 27 year old black male, who was found inside of an SUV with an undisclosed amount of illegal narcotics and other drug paraphernalia. The deceased was identified as Rayford Green and was found at 3:46 am in the parking lot of Egg Roll on Devine Street. Anyone with information is asked to call Crime Stoppers."

"We also have some disturbing news involving Narcotics Agent, Brian Steeples. Steeples is currently under investigation and

faces charges for robbery, extortion, conspiracy, and assault. Vinson Tibbs is pressing charges on Steeples, alleging that Steeples robbed him of $1200, took some marijuana from him, and forced him to sell crack cocaine after shooting him. Tibbs stated that Steeples threatened to kill him if he told anyone or didn't sell the product. Several witnesses have come forth to corroborate Tibbs's claims. Tibbs admits to being a minor marijuana dealer, but he says he told Mr. Steeples he was afraid to deal with crack. After he was shot, Mr. Tibbs knew the situation was out of his hands. He called the authorities while waiting on an ambulance to treat his gunshot wound. Steeples is also a suspect in the home invasion that occurred in the Willow Run Project where his partner, Narcotics Agent, Nicholas Turner, was killed by Andre Major. It was said that Turner was off duty, didn't have a badge with him, was carrying a 9 mm., which had shaved serial numbers, and was wearing a mask. Andre Major is being held at the Alvin S. Glenn Detention Center..."

Major couldn't believe what he'd just heard. His mind had to be playing tricks on him. He pinched his forearm as hard as he could. He had to be dreaming, but the congratulatory comments being thrown at him revealed that he was wide awake.

"Major, you bout to blow this bitch!" he heard someone say.

Major was relieved to hear the good news. His confidence was restored after hearing the news briefing. The weight of the world had been taken off his shoulders. He wondered if Brian Steeples was the same narco who'd been robbing his workers. When he got out, he was definitely going to find out now that he had a name.

All Major could think about was getting payback on all those who turned their backs on him. Miguel, Mook, and Fresh was at the top of his list.

As they sat in Applebee's, they looked like a perfectly happy family. Since Major was gone, Kimiko and her son were spending time with the man who treated her like shit.

She felt like maybe they had a chance to make things work. "Baby, this salmon is delicious," Kimiko said.

"Yeah, this shrimp alfredo is what's happenin' though."

"Look at my son, he seems to really be enjoying them fries."

"I just wish we could do this every day for the rest of our lives," Kimiko said as she looked at Brian with love.

"And who says we can't?" Brian replied. "It won't hurt to start over. Are you with that?" he asked.

"I don't know what the future holds. I saw the news, Brian. Do you think these charges will hold up in a court of law? Are the things they saying about you true?"

"Baby let's not discuss this in front of BJ. Right now, all I wanna talk about is us being a family. Are you with it or not?"

"I understand, and If you're serious, I would love to. It's all I've ever wanted, for us to be together as a unit, " she said, falling for the bait.

Hearing that was music to his ears. Kimiko had his heart, but he knew they could never truly be a family. The chips were stacked against him. Under different circumstances, Kimiko would've been *the* one, but right now, he had entirely too much going on.

"Baby, let's take it slow and get to know each other again and work towards being a couple. I would really love to give us a chance," he said.

Kimiko blushed, feeling like she was finally getting what she'd been praying for. She looked at her cell phone and knew that it had to be Major calling from a private number.

I'm sorry Major, but I can't answer right now. I have a chance at saving my family, and I know you would want the best for me, she said to herself, pressing the end button as she continued to enjoy her fantasy and time with Brian.

*****

"Damn, baby! Why you ain't answering' yo' phone?" Mook asked.

"It ain't nobody but Major," Selah replied. "I don't feel like hearing his bullshit. There's nothing I can do for him now."

"The next time he call, let me answer it," Mook said, trying to act tough, knowing he didn't want to fan flames with Major .

As they sat in the living room bagging up weed by the pounds, *knock! Knock!*

Selah stood up and walked to the door peering through the peep hole. Then, she opened it when she noticed who it was.

"What up y'all?" Big Ram said, as he walked his oversized self in Selah's apartment. His shoulders were so wide he damn near needed to turn sideways to enter the apartment.
"Y'all think y'all got enough shit in here?"

"What's up, Hammer Head?" Selah said, calling him by the name she'd been using since they were younger.

"Did y'all see the news?"

"Nah, why? What happened?" Mook asked as he weighed some weed and handed it to Selah to bag up.

"They say Major might get out because those narcos were dirty and off duty. Plus, the dude who Major killed, his partner is under investigation for all kinds of robberies and other shit. They gone burn his ass just cause he black too, watch and see."

"Yeah, whatever! But Major's ass ain't never gettin' outta jail. They offered that nigga the death penalty for killing that white boy. The rope is already tied tight around his neck. Nigga might as well jump," Mook said.

"I hear ya', but remember I told you, and I don't want no part of what's gon' happen when he gets out. Major always played fair with us. Why so much animosity towards the nigga who put us in the game?"

"Whatever, scary ass nigga! We was already in the game. That nigga ain't did shit for me that I didn't pay for. Just grab them two pounds and take them to Lil Vint in Ames Manor," Mook demanded.

"Oh, hell nah! That's the lil' nigga who pressin' charges on the dirty narco they been talkin' 'bout on the news. The water around that nigga is boiling hot, and I ain't getting burned fa' nobody. Fuck that shit. Call me when I got to traffic to somebody else," Big Ram replied with finality.

Selah burst out laughing. As big as Ram was, she didn't think he was afraid of shit.

Mook curled his lip and cut his eyes at Ram. "Nigga get yo' scary ass outta here then. I'll handle that shit my damn self. Yo' big ass probably scared of your own shadow. Damn shame, you got all that weight on you and can't do shit with it. Come on, baby. Ride with me."

Mook left a few pounds of smoke at Selah's apartment and took the rest to his stash house on Westbrook Avenue off of North Main Street.

He pulled out and headed to Lil' Vint, driving up Prescott Road. When he pulled up, Vint was posted in his mom's hallway.

He saw Mook, limped towards the car, and hopped in the back seat. Selah handed him the Macy's bag containing the weed.

Vint handed her the cash, and Selah rapidly counted out $2200 as if her ass worked at a bank.

"Man, Vint, what I hear bout you had a run in wit a dirty narco?" Mook asked.

"Yeah! This nigga with dreads tried to extort me. The nigga shot me and handed me a crack pack. My mama and a few neighbors witnessed that shit and called the police. They told me to press charges, so I did, but we good. You know I ain't on no po-po type shit. I'ma make they ass pay me for what that nigga did. Bet that," Vint replied.

"I hear you, lil' bruh. Just be safe and fuck with me. I got plenty more of that fire weed," Mook bragged, trying to sound like he was the boss, but neither of them noticed the white Challenger with dark tint parked behind them.

When Mook pulled off, the person in the Challenger watched which apartment he entered with the package, then they tailed Mook back to Willow Runs.

Mook's phone had been ringing off the hook since they went to meet Vint, but he was ignoring the calls because he already knew who it was. Trina, a female he met a few weeks ago, was blowing his shit up. He had fucked her a few times and tricked a coupla dollars, now she was acting obsessive, but none of that mattered cause her sex game was insane and Mook had to figure out a way to shake Selah for a few hours so he could tap that.

Mook pulled into Selah's parking lot like they ain't have a care in the world. He had that DMG Cip, "Drip" blasting loudly as he exited the car stunting.

"All this blue cheese on me, I got dip baby. All this water on me, I got drip baby," he rapped arrogantly putting on a show for the hood hoes. He bounced to and fro, popping his collar and shit- showboating.

Mook turned off the ignition, then opened the door, but forgot to pocket the money he just made. The dude in the Challenger witnessed him with the bankroll in his hand as he stuffed it in his pocket. He was sizing Mook up by his royal blue 87' Chevy Caprice, with the 26-inch matching rims.

As they walked towards Selah's apartment, Von watched them from the brick wall. He hated the way his sister was handling Major. After all Major did for them, Von wanted to rob and kill Mook so bad, but Major told him he'd handle that when he got out of jail. Even though he was facing the Death Penalty, Von knew that Major was smart and strong enough to wiggle out of his situation. He always did, so he relaxed like his partner asked. When Selah and Mook went into the apartment, Von focused on the Challenger that had backed in by the 17 building and was just sitting there. He wasn't worried because him or his homies had nothing on them but their guns, and not even the police was going to have a chance to get too close. Von knew right then that Mook was hot. He just hoped it wasn't the feds because he didn't want his sister tied up in Mook's bullshit. Von was about to have one of the smokers take a look closer to see who was in the Challenger, when suddenly they decided to pull off.

"Baby, I gotta make a run right quick, ok?" Mook said.

"Whatever, Mook! That shit don't sound right. I hope you takin' that dope and weed with you because you know it done been in here too damn long. I was taught not to shit where you lay," Selah said with attitude.

"I ain't gon' be gone but a few hours, so pump yo' breaks," Mook countered, getting a little offended by her saying what she was taught. He didn't give a damn about her street education or Major for that matter.

"You one hard headed nigga! Now I see what Major meant by niggas are careless. If the po-po come in here, this yo' shit because I'm tellin' you to take the shit with you," she concurred adamantly.

"Selah, watch yo' fuckin' mouth because I ain't Major, and why would the po-po come here? They got all them niggas outside to fuck with. Them people ain't thinkin' 'bout you."

"The same way they came in here when Major killed one of they asses. And I bet you ain't even notice that white Challenger follow us from Ames Manor, did you? Nigga, I was taught by the best."

"Well, maybe you need to go and get the best outta jail."

"Don't worry, he'll be out soon, but nigga, get yo' dope and get the fuck out or I 'm gon' give that shit away. Watch me," she threatened. Selah had grown tired of Mook's bullshit. She regretted ever fucking with him. Mook was prideful and loud, always had to make noise and put on a show.

"Whatever, Selah! I'll be back," Mook said as he walked out, slamming the door behind him.

*****

When Brian entered the precinct, all conversations ceased and every eye fell on him.

"Fuck y'all looking at?" he grunted before taking a seat behind his desk. Before he could park his ass good, the chief of police called his name from the doorway of his office.

"Steeples get your ass in my office, now!"

The whispers and chatter of his colleagues resumed and could be heard as he stood from his desk and walked towards the chief's office.

Brian entered the office, closing the door behind him. A look of anger and disappointment covered the police chief's face. The chief stood behind the desk with his knuckles on top of it, his rotund belly strained against the bottoms of his uniform shirt.

"What's going on, chief? You seem upset."

"Steeples don't waltz your ass into my office and act as if you don't know what the fuck is going on! Your face has been plastered across every news outlet all goddamn day. I've got the DOJ breathing down my neck about that shit you pulled out in the field. There's video evidence of the entire ordeal taking place in Ames Manor! Tell me what in the flying fuck you were thinking?"

Brian dropped his head. A suitable response couldn't escape his lips. With so much going on across the nation with officers killing black men and planting drugs on them, Brian knew that any words used to defend his actions would come across as nonsense. Chief wouldn't understand the reasoning behind his actions, so he kept his mouth closed.

"You have nothing to say for yourself? Steeples you've engaged in criminal acts of public corruption that erode the confidence that people have in law enforcement. You and your team of henchmen have lost your goddamn minds!"

"I know I fucked up, Chief, but it's not what it looks like-" was all Brian could say in his defense.

Chief held his palm up in a dismissive manner. "The trust I placed on you to work that area was instilled because I thought you would obey the oath to conduct yourself in an ethical manner. The creed you pledged to become an officer, you've made a mockery of. For that, I cannot and will not have you on my force. From this point forward, you are being placed on suspension without pay. Maybe some of the drug money you've made will keep you afloat. Steeples, you disgrace me and other members of law enforcement who pledged to honor and protect civilians. You're a wolf in sheep's clothing, and I don't care for your kind. Out of my office. Your presence is making me nauseous!"

Ride or Run

Mook's cell phone rang repeatedly, nonstop. "Goddamn. Do that shit, baby. Fuck that phone," Trina had his meat locked within the confines of her jaws. This was some of the best neck he'd ever had. He couldn't will himself to stop her.

He played in her box as she topped him off. One finger, then two, slid into her drenched opening. Trina's phat monkey suctioned his fingers. Her cream saturating his hand and ran down her meaty thigh. Sexy moans escaped her lips before she allowed his Johnson to plop out of her mouth.

Coming up for air, she smacked her lips. "Nigga, you need to get that. Shit fuckin' up my groove," Trina said before going back down on him. With his eyes rolling in the back of his head, his toes curled, and his hands holding on

to the arms of the recliner, Mook could do nothing but enjoy the pleasure of a lifetime.

Her oral game had his young ass stuttering, "sh-sh-shiiit! Girl, ain't... nothin' . .mo'. . important than what's happenin . . . right now!" he replied.

While teasing the head of Mook's dick, licking around and under his balls, "it might be something serious. Don't nobody call back to back like that unless shit real. My mouth ain't going nowhere and this dick ain't either, so, handle yo' business," Trina said as she finally stopped. She loved being in control, but she hated a weak nigga at the same time. If he missed money, that would be less she'd be able to get from him later.

"Girl, why you stop?"

"Because, you need to answer yo' phone and make sho' nothin' is wrong with yo' family or close friends! Don't need to be missin' no money either. It's expensive to play in my pussy." she responded seriously.

Mook noticed her seriousness and realized that she was right. He looked at his phone which had over twenty missed calls. He called his mother's house first. "Boy, where you at?" she yelled in the phone.

"At a friend's house, why? What's goin' on, ma?"

"The po-po kicked in Selah's door and is about to lock her up for some shit she said was yours. She said either you come claim yo' shit, or she's telling on you because you won't answer yo' phone. "

"What you mean, is about to lock her up?" he asked.

"Like I said, about to! They at her apartment waitin' on you to call her, so you can come claim the drugs in her apartment."

"Ma, what should I do?" he asked sounding like the momma's boy he was.

"Mook, I can't say. That's a tough one right there. Either way it goes, the drugs are in her house and in her possession. If you come and claim' em, they gon' lock both of y'all up."

"Alright, I'll figure some'n out."

"These ain't my drugs. All this shit belongs to Mook. I can call him. He'll tell y'all this his shit," Selah snitched trying to save herself, but they weren't trying to hear anything she had to say.

The officers chuckled. "Ma'am, we want to believe you, but this is your apartment and you knowingly have illegal substances in here," one of them stated.

She saw the other one roll his eyes. "That nigga is not coming here to claim this shit. Mirandize her, so we can go."

Selah immediately started crying. "No, he will. He's coming watch and see."

The officer cuffed her while reading Miranda's at the same time. She was charged with trafficking 250 grams of cocaine, and five pounds of marijuana. While she was in the county, she tried calling Mook for two days straight, but received no answer.

Selah loved hanging out with Mook and being a part of his everyday hustle. Even though he wasn't making nowhere near what Major made, she enjoyed being seen around the well-known hustlers. Being in their company made her feel as if she were a part of something, but at the same time, now she understood why Major kept her at a distance while he handled his business. He was only protecting her from situations like this one. She used to think he wanted all the fame, but now she saw the bigger picture. Major really cared for her wellbeing while Mook didn't give a fuck about her. He only had relations with her to prove a point: that he could fuck the boss's bitch. She thought she was using Mook, but Mook was using her ass.

Good thing her little brother Von saw what went down. He paid her bond as soon as she was given one. She was given a $50,000 bond. Her lawyer said that she was facing up to 20 years in prison, if found guilty. Now, all Selah could think about was Major and the way he loved, provided, and protected her. She promised herself to give him a surprise visit the first chance she got and to give Mook all the hell he deserved.

"Can't believe I'm losing my apartment behind that nigga." she mumbled while packing her things. Von walked in with a crazy, disgusted look on his face. She looked up at him, then quickly back down to what she was doing. Feelings of shame washed over her. She could see the disappointed look in Von's eyes.

"Selah, I love you, but I hate the way you handled big bruh while he's gone. All Major ever did was look out for us, and you repay him by fuckin' with one of his workers, a disloyal one at that. You know better, and I don't know what you were thinkin', or if you were thinkin' at all. Major would've never let you go down behind his shit, but know this, the only thing that stopped me from killin' Mook is that he owe Major money.

"Well, what was I supposed to do? Major ain't neva gettin' outta jail. Mook was the only person who helped me since Major been gone."

Von jerked his neck back as if Selah were about to hit him. "Girl, you can't be serious. The nigga was helpin' you with Major's money, which is what he was supposed to do as Major's homie, not fuck his girl. You were supposed to be Major's boss bitch but look at you now. Major ain't fuckin' with you no more when he comes home, and he will come home, you watch. Now you gotta get a job and accept what little help I throw yo' way or start back trickin' off with whatever dope boy who gonna allow you to get close to 'em. You had it made. Couldn't keep ya' legs closed for five fuckin' minutes before you started layin' up with that nickel and dime hustla," he tossed at her with five of his fingers held up in her face.

"Look at how the bitch nigga handled you. Left yo' ass back there in county to rot. He didn't give a fuck if you posted bond or not. Nigga in hidin' because he thinks I'm lookin' for him, but it's outta my hands."

Selah exhaled deeply. She didn't expect her brother to come down on her so harshly, even though everything he said was true. "Well, I'll be alright, and if Major does come home, he ain't gon' leave me. I got him whipped."

"Girl, you don't even see the bigger picture. Pussy don't make a nigga's heart pump. That passed through box of yours don't please a real nigga. Loyalty do. You lost that man's respect by fuckin' with a bottom feeder. Lost that man's respect because you couldn't uphold yo' dignity. You just proved that yo' ass is just like these other scallywags out here. Sister or not, that was ho' shit. After all the years of knowin' Major, you still don't understand his loyalty to us, but you will never have him like you once had. Sis, I've paid yo' first coupla months' rent, so get up on yo' shit," Von gave her a hug and bounced. As soon as the door closed behind him, emotion took over and Selah let out a gut wrenching scream before tears ran down her face.

Major still couldn't believe what he saw on the news a few days ago. His heart rate accelerated, and goosebumps covered his body as thoughts of freedom took over him. He wanted to call Selah, but he felt there was no hope. He always told her about shitting where she laid. Major wanted to help her, but she needed to learn this lesson all by herself. He told Von to find her an apartment and pay the rent for a few months, then see what she was going to do for herself.

He loved her, but not enough to let her bring him down. Bad enough, she left him for dead. He was never calling her to complain about anything she was doing or what he'd heard. All he needed for her to do was stop by a few of Miguel's spots and see if he could pull some strings for him, but she refused to answer her phone or respond to his letters.
He had Majesty and his cousin Kim trying to contact Miguel, but his family said he was out of town. After a few months, Major understood that Miguel was hiding out, afraid that Major would turn snitch on him. Obviously, he didn't know Major too well because Major's mind was far from snitching. He wanted to fight the law the right way. Things were looking really good for Major.

All he had to do was hold on a little while longer.

Kimiko was supposed to be coming to see him today, but she never showed. It was one disappointment after another with the women in his life. He was a little torn up about the way he was being treated by her and Selah. "Inmate Major, visit!" the CO's voice echoed throughout the dorm.

Maybe she came after all. Major walked to the visiting booth, but he was shocked to see Quies. She wasn't even on his visitation list, but anybody who knew Quies knew that she could be very conniving and convincing.

"What's up, Quies? What you doin' here?" Major asked, giving her a winning smile. Never in a million years did he expect to see her. Truth be told, he was happy for a visit from whomever right about now as mentally disturbed as he was.

"How are you doin' in here?" she asked. "I'm surprised you're not out yet, knowing the way your mind works. I saw that shit on the news. You'll blow this spot in no time," she said, ignoring his question, smiling that pretty smile he was always so attracted to.

Quies, Major, Selah, and Fresh all went to school together. Major and Quies kicked it on the low, but once her and Fresh got involved, they decided to stay on the hush about their dealings. Fresh fell in love, and being that Fresh was his partner since elementary, Major decided to let him be happy, but Quies never quite got over Major.

"What do I owe this visit, Quies?" he asked again.

"I was just thinking about you, as always. You know how I feel about you, and I hate the way Fresh and Selah are treatin' you. You and Fresh supposed to be better than that. At least, that's what I thought."

"Yeah, but that's life. People reveal themselves when you're placed in a fucked up situation. To be honest, I anticipated the shit, but it's cool. You can never make someone be the way you want them to be, especially when you're not around. Outta sight, outta mind is a true saying, and I respect it."

"Well, I want you to know that I'm always here if you need me. Major, I love you, and you don't deserve the deceit from your so-called friends. You should see Fresh out there spending money on cars, jewelry, and women like there's no tomorrow. Him and your lil' brothers are all at this new club called

Insomnia every weekend like they own it, with their flashy cars parked out front. Niggas think they rappers."

"Flashy cars?"

"Yeah, Major. You didn't know?"

"Nah, this my first time hearing about the cars," Major said greedy for the details Quies was about to feed him.

"Boy, oh-boy! Yo' brothers got all kinda hooked up cars with the big rims on them. The young boy Dip do too, and Fresh is just outta control. He bought a Challenger on some big rims, and he got me a 750 LI, and he finally got me my beauty salon. Plus, he got a Escalade. Everybody ridin' high and fly."

"What about Von?" Major asked, just soaking it all in.

"You know Von acts just like you. He don't even be around them like that. He still hangin' in the hood playin' broke, but I know he's caked up because Selah said when Mook wouldn't get her outta jail, Von did and he put her in a nice house in Crane Forest."

"Quies, if Fresh is lookin' out for you, why you tellin' me what he's doin' wrong?"

"Nigga, I work hard for mine, and I know you worked hard for yours. I just don't like how he's treatin' you after all you've established for him. He never talk about you, and when I ask about you, he can't even tell me your status. He acts like he don't want you to beat your charge, so he can spend all yo' money. He buyin' coke from Big Geno, who Selah be fuckin behind you and Mook's back with her hot ass. When you beat yo' charge, you need to get with me, on the real though."

"You know I can't do that, but I appreciate you keepin' me on my toes about everything. I'll make sho' I stay in contact with you though, ok. Maybe we can go out together sometimes, as friends. I know Fresh is acting up, but the nigga loves you."
With that being said, they ended their visit. Major had a lot on his mind, and shit
wasn't going to be the same when he got out.

These Hoes Ain't Loyal

"Vito! Vito!" his girl yelled from the living room.

Waking up from a deep sleep, "why you yellin' my damn name like you goin' crazy?"

"Come'ere! Ms. Pat want you!"

He thought he heard her wrong for a second until he walked in the living room to see the next door neighbor.

"Hey, Ms. Pat."

"Hey, Vito. I just wanted to tell you that you need to be more careful with the way you handle yo' business when you go under yo' hood. I saw you around four this mornin'. I coulda been the wrong person and called the po-po on yo' crazy ass. Why you be hidin' that big ass gun under yo' hood, anyway?"

"What you doin' up that time of mornin', Ms. Pat?"

"There you go tryna mind grown folks bitness. Just learn to handle yo' shit different. Eyes are always open round here, you hear me? Hazel next doe to me will have yo' ass comin' up with bond money. You hear me?"

"Yes, ma'am. Thank you," Vito said, then went back to the bedroom to get dressed. He had to help Fresh get rid of the dope he had.

Ms. Pat and Neeko talked for a few while Vito got dressed.

The Colony Projects was live like always when Vito walked to the 800 building to post up with his Blood homies. Even though he wasn't in the gang, he was tight with them because they grew up together.

As Vito stood on the porch of his boy Vamp, he noticed Trina's Escalade pull into the 600 parking lot. Sayso hopped in the truck for a few minutes, then hopped back out. *Now what the fuck she doing out here with this nigga Sayso? Bitches ain't shit. I swear.* Vito tilted his head to get a better view of the vehicle. After confirming it was indeed her, he nodded.

He had plans on finding out one way or another.

Vito, Vamp and a few of the other homies stood around smoking on some loud while knocking back a fifth of Henny.

Sayso walked towards them but was stopped by a serve on the way. When he got to the crowd, Vito was about to ask how he knew Trina until Vamp said something to Sayso.

"Damn, Say... I thought you ain't have no more work?"

"I still had a few pieces left from the last pack, but my cousin just came through and dropped me a few ounces off. I need you to hit the kitchen for me right quick, I got you," Sayso said.

"Aight. Let me holla at my girl first. I'll be right back," Vamp said, as he walked in the apartment they were posted in front of.

Vito just sat back and soaked it all in. He wanted to know what was on Fresh's mind, serving the homies in the hood behind his back when he had shit on lock already.

"Yo. Say, Vito, y'all step in right quick. The rest of y'all, fall back for a minute and watch the streets," Vamp said.

Vamp had two Pyrex jars on the table, along with a digital scale, and baking soda. Sayso handed him the cocaine while Vamp was weighing it up. Vito was ready to see how it looked. They were the only ones with that fish scale a pinkish color like this. It was a small drought, but Major had left them loaded.

"Damn, bruh, this look like the same shit you be havin'," Vamp said to Vito.

Vito already knew it was the same shit, but he played it off. "Yeah, it do, don't it?"

"My cousin be hittin' some nigga up who be stashin' at her house. She let me help her out at a unbelievable price," Sayso bragged.

"Oh, yeah? So, yo' cousin is Trina, huh?" Vito said not being able to hold in what he knew any longer it.

"Nigga, this me and my partner shit."

"What the fuck you talkin' bout, Vito?" Sayso asked, wishing he would've kept his mouth shut.

"Vamp just keep workin' yo' magic. Let me make a quick call to verify this shit. If I'm wrong, I apologize, but my nigga, I know how our product look. Plus, I just saw the Escalade my partner bought Trina pull outta yo' parking lot," Vito said, as he dialed Fresh's number and put it on speaker phone.

"Yoo! What up, bruh, " Fresh answered.

"Bruh, where you at.?

"I'm at my boo spot. Why?"

"I want you to check yo' stash and tell me what's missin'."

Fresh went to the back room to his safe. He looked in it and was shocked to see that the scale weighed only five ounces.

"Oh, shit, bruh. I had a jar of them cookies, all kinds too. You must've been over here with'cho greedy ass?" he replied speaking in code.

"Yo' boo is stealin' from you, nigga, but don't worry, I got it back. Just handle yo' end."

"Alright, bruh. Thanks," Fresh said, then he hung up the phone, not believing what he'd just found out.

"I knew some'n wasn't right with you havin' all that damn money and never leaving the hood. Nigga, you was broke as fuck a few months ago. Around the same time, my dawg claimed he was losin' cash, but you and Trina's stank ass was comin' up off our shit."

"Man, Vito, I ain't know, dawg. You can have that dope back, but, man, tell yo' boy not to hurt my cousin."

"Nigga, you or yo' cousin don't call no shots. You been getting on and wouldn't even show yo' dawgs in the hood no love when they were fucked up, but we 'bout to go to yo' spot and see what yo' stash lookin' like right now. Stand up, nigga."

Vito pulled out his Luger 9mm and pointed it at Sayso. "Nigga, it betta be at least forty grand in this bitch, or I'ma leave yo' ass twitching," he gritted.

Vito had one of the homies to drive them to Sayso's baby mama's house in Bayberry. They went in the house to his safe and to Vito's surprise, Sayso had sixty grand. He took fifty from the safe.

"Man, I thought you said I owed y'all forty grand?" Sayso whined.

Whap! Vito chopped him in the head with his weapon. Sayso stumbled while grabbing the gash that zig zagged down the middle of his head. "Pussy ass nigga, tape yo' nuts up, bitch ass. This extra for the trouble, worry, and heartache you caused us. You better be glad I'm leavin' you with some'n to get right with."

"Damn, alright, man."

Vito and his driver walked out of the house, but before he closed the door, "Nigga, I bet not hear nothin' about what just happened, or I'm gon' take it as a threat."

Fresh searched the entire apartment after what Vito told him. He couldn't believe Trina's betrayal. At least Quies never stole from him. Fresh looked everywhere he thought there was a stash, but Trina was smarter than he thought. After calculating how much money he felt was missing from his stash, it had to be well over fifty grand because he was missing four ounces here and there each time. He always thought maybe it was the liquor and pills, but he'd been doing this shit for years now and never came up that short. He thought maybe his balling habits had really gotten out of control, but it was Trina stealing from him all along. He'd found a little over ten grand, but he knew she had more stashed somewhere else. He had to come up with a plan, get some of his money back, and then leave the bitch.

When Trina finally came home, he told her that he had to go out of town to get back straight with a new connect. She was all for it because she knew that it would only be more money to steal and stash. Trina had plans on starting her own business. She wanted to open a massage parlor, and Fresh was going to unknowingly be her financial investor.

Later that night, Trina sat in her living room masturbating while watching Superhead's porno video. She was fully naked with a 12" dildo damn near all the way inside her shaven pussy. Her hand was between her knees while her manicured toes were planted on the couch cushions. She was about to have another orgasm until her front door came off the hinges after one kick. *Boom!*

The two masked men entered with guns pointed at her. She threw her hands in the air and left the dildo inside her slimy wet pussy, but it slowly slid out of her deep tunnel, landing close to her feet with a plop.

"Bitch, where the dope and money at?" the short chubby one said.

"It ain't no dope or money in here," she replied.

"Ok, this bitch wanna play games," the slim one said.

He walked up on her. *Whap! Whap! Smack!* A three piece dropped her to the floor.

"Bruh, tie that bitch up since she wanna play games!" He grabbed her by the wrists, turned her on her back, and tied her up with the zip ties while the other one plugged up the iron that was sitting in the corner of her kitchen floor.

Blood dripped from her nose and into her mouth as tears flooded her eyes. "Please, it's nothing in here."

"Yeah, bruh, turn that iron on high because if this bitch don't start talkin', I'ma stick that hot mufucka right to the side of her face. Then start by plucking her toe nails from her pretty ass toes," he said, as he pulled the pliers from his back pocket.

"Oh, hell no. Y'all ain't gotta do all that," she muttered though busted lips. "I got some money in the rim of the curtains ova there." She pointed towards the curtains behind a love seat couch.

The slim robber tip toed and ran his fingers across the top of the curtains until he felt the lump in the far right corner of the curtains. He had to take the curtains down on that side and grab the zip lock bag from the seams of them. "Damn, girl! How much money this is?" the chubby one asked.

"That's thirty thousand."

"Bitch, you got some more in here, all them ballers you fuck wit," the slim one countered.

"I swear that's it! Please y'all, I ain't got nothin' else!"

"Alright, bitch, I believe you," Slim said. "Aye, bruh, let's roll."

Chubby hesitated, drooling from the mouth looking at her pretty pussy. "Damn, you gotta phat pussy."

He kneeled down, sticking two, three, then four fingers inside of her wet tunnel.

"Please, don't. I gave y'all all I have. Please don't rape me," Trina cried.

Whap!

"Bitch, hush! All that damn whining. I was just playing with the shit. Don't want none of this pussy after that big ass dildo fell out. I can probably hear ma'self echo in that box," he grunted before standing and kicking her in the cat with all his might.

Arrrghhhh! Trina hollered as she balled into a knot.

Yes, Your Majesty...

Kim handed the last customer their receipt from the $50 Boost phone minute card, locked the door, turned on her store closed sign, then walked to the employee lounge area. Majesty was checking herself out in the full body mirror, which Major had personally put on the wall for times he and Majesty sexed there.

"Girl! Look at you! Acting like you're going on a date, with yo' hot ass," Kim said.

"Girl, I just want to look enticing and delicious for my husband. Some'n wrong with that?" Majesty asked as she talked to Kim while still admiring her backside in some skin tight black G-Star denims. She also donned Cubannie Link earrings and ring, Funky Fanny's mink hat, and G-Star shirt and jacket.

"You know you're too much, " Kim said.

"I gotta go and help relieve my baby's stress. Them other whores ain't hittin' on shit, so wifey gotta step up."

"I hear that, girl, " Kim said as she glanced at her vibrating cell phone. "Girl, let me see who this is blowin' up my line."

"Excuse me, Majesty. This Quies."

"I wonder what she want?" Majesty questioned as she applied gloss to her lips.

"Hello?" Kim answered, but got no response right then.

All she heard was a dude's voice in the background. "Who the fuck is Brian, huh, Quies? That's yo' new nigga?" Kim looked at the phone, "Quies? Quies?" she said into her phone.

"Hello? Kim!" Quies said in the phone.

"Quies, what's goin' on with you, girl? You alright?" Kim asked in a concerned manner.

"Kim, can you please come pick me up from Dutch Square Mall. I'm tired of Fresh putting' his fuckin' hands on me and threatening to take his truck back. Fuck him and this truck-owww...Ahhh! Ack! Ack! Oh, hell no, Fresh... Stop, Fresh! Kim, please come get me." She yelled as she cried into the phone, then the line went dead.

"Majesty, I gotta get to Quies before Fresh kill her. Tell my cousin I said what's up and enjoy yo' visit," Kim said as she rushed to the door.

"Oh, yeah, Majesty, lockup for me."

"I got you, girl. Handle yo' business and drive safe."

*****

"What's up with all this texting "I miss you" messages and shit? You miss that nigga? Huh, Quies?" Fresh asked, as he backhand slapped her with his left hand while she was still driving. She swerved into the right lane and almost hit the Honda next to them, but Fresh quickly grabbed the wheel and guided their Tahoe back into the proper lane to avoid causing an accident.

"Fresh, why are you acting so fuckin' childish? You gon' fuck around and get us killed or locked up!" Quies said while crying, flinching each time he moved his hands afraid of being struck again.

"Because, I don't give a fuck! Especially when you out there givin' away my pussy!"

"The last I checked, you left me and moved in with yo' other bitch, so fuck you, Fresh," she said as she drove toward the mall.

"Oh, it's fuck me?" he punched Quies in the face. Her head smacked against the driver's side window as she slammed on the breaks in the middle of traffic.

They were right in front of Jiffy Lube on Broad River Road. She rushed out of the car while trying to dial Brian's number at the same time. Fresh got out and chased her, almost being hit by oncoming traffic. Quies ran across the street to McDonald's, attempting to make it to the mall to meet Kim, but Fresh was too fast for her. He caught up to her in no time. By this time, she was leaving Brian a message because the call went to his voice mail.

Fresh heard what she was saying and grew angrier. "Oh, you tryna call yo' nigga to save you, huh, bitch?" he said while dragging her by her hair. "That's what I want! Tell that nigga he can meet with me if he want some. You my bitch, and I'll murk one of these niggas in them streets behind what's mine."

"I wish he would answer his phone because Brian would fuck yo' punk, woman beatin' ass up!" Quies said as she tried pulling Fresh's hands out of her hair, while trying to avoid the concrete of McDonald's parking lot skinning up her ass and back. He had her in a full Nelson, half walking, half dragging her back to the truck.

Fresh popped her in the head twice with his free hand. "Shut up wit yo' hoein' ass. You ain't satisfied 'til a nigga beatin' the shit outta you. Gotta treat you like a fuckin child since you think I'm to be played with!"

Fresh was so lost in the scuffle with Quies that he was oblivious to the crowd of onlookers that had grown in the parking lot, the halt of backed up traffic, and the five county police cars that were pulling in.

"Release the woman and place your hands above your head! Do it now!" an officer yelled through the speakers.

Fresh released Quies from the full Nelson but not before taking his foot and kicking her to the ground. She flew face first into the pavement, busting up her knees and hands while trying to break her fall.

Three officers tazed Fresh at once. The electricity from the shocks caused him to fall backwards with his arms outstretched, as if he were falling into a pool.

Boom! It sounded like a car crash as his body collided with the trunk of a parked car before his body hit the ground...

*****

Instead of sitting around trading war stories, playing cards, dominoes, and other jail bullshit, Major studied his real estate books and blue printed ways to attract more money to his club. Every day after a few hours of studying and planning, he would work out to keep his body in top shape. Then, he would shower and relax.

Even with the death penalty looming over his head, Major didn't allow his circumstances to distract him. Every night before bed, he meditated on a positive outcome involving his case. Major understood that thoughts became things. Daily, he envisioned life outside the confinements of jail and knew that soon, they'd become a reality.

Major wasn't worried at all. He knew the law. The most they could rightfully charge him with was unlawful carrying of a firearm. He'd been down six months and wasn't going to ever give up on himself or let the system railroad him to cover their officers' sloppy mistakes.

As Major stood in the shower pulling on his wood, he heard the officer call his name under the spray of water.

"He in the shower, I'll get 'em," he heard his celly say.

Major was in a zone, taking his time caressing his love muscle while thinking of past sexcapades with different women, but after hearing his name called, he decided to go ahead and quickly jack himself off before he lost his groove. He had a dangerous stroke going on. He thought about the loud moans Kimiko made when he fucked her in the craziest positions, and, to top it off, he could never get enough of Majesty's small frame, with the fattest, tightest, wettest, warmest pussy he ever had. Just the thought of that pleasurable combination, caused his knees to buckle as an explosive orgasm ripped through his pipe. One hand pressed the shower wall to brace himself from buckling, and his other hand still massaged his manhood. Major was so zoned out, he forgot where he was. Until he opened his eyes and looked at the lingerie pictures he had stuck to the wall of Kimiko, Selah, and Majesty.

"Fuck," he grumbled in frustration. "Lemme get my perverted ass out this damn shower."

He turned off the shower, dried off, got dressed, grabbed his pictures from the wall, and went to his cell. He got himself together, then went to see what the officers wanted.

"Inmate Major, you have a visit," the officer said.

"Ok, that's what's up!" he replied, then headed to see who was popping up on him.

Major really didn't want a visit. He had planned on studying a little harder today, but when he saw Majesty in all her glory, he lit up from the inside out.

"Hey there, handsome," she said, still standing so he could take in her attire and get a good look at her physique.

"Yes, your Majesty. Turn around so daddy can get a better look at all that sexy goodness. Damn, baby! You lucky I done jacked off already. Them tight ass jeans make a nigga horny all over again!"

"Boy, you so stupid!" she said, blushing at his comment.

"So, what's on ya' mind?"

"I just wanted to see my husband, that's all."

"Thanks, baby. So, is everythang good with business?"

"Everythang is everythang. You know how I do. Did Cybil come see you yet? She has good news baby."

"Nah, why? What's up?"

"You bout to be a free man."

"You bullshittin'!"

"I don't play games, but she called yesterday and said she was working something out to have you out sometime this week. You coming home, baby. It's almost over."

While they were conversing, Cybil walked up behind Majesty with a big pretty smile on her face.

"Speaking of the devil," Major said.

"What's up y'all?" Cybil said. "Well, I 'm not goin' to beat around the bush. Major, your case was thrown out. The shooting was ruled justified, so you're a free man, but it may take a day or two for me to get the paper work processed."

"Stop bullshittin', Cybil! I ain't up for no jokes right now."

"Andre, what did I just say? I also want you to know that one of the narcotics who was with the victim is still out there. He's known for doing sneaky, dirty shit, and he might want some get back, so I need for you to be extra careful upon release. You could possibly have a target on your back."

"You know I can handle myself."

"I don't doubt that, but you don't know who he is. Yet, he knows who you are. I want you to stop by my office as soon as you get out, ok, " she said, giving him a look only he could read.

"Oh yeah? I'll be there," he replied. "Cybil, see if you can stop the media from broadcasting my arrival, ok?"

"I can handle that," she said and excused herself.

Major and Majesty shared a few more words, then they ended their visit also. She left feeling like the happiest woman alive. She just prayed that he stayed free.

This Life We Livin', Got Us All Meetin' Up In Prison...

After his visits, he did exactly what he planned to do, study. He was prepared to give real estate a chance. It would really help out a lot with the plans he had. He was tired of the dope game. Yet hustling was all he knew, but if buying and selling houses was anything like Kimiko mentioned, he was about to fall in love with his new grind.

As he sat back thinking deeply about his new goals, his thoughts were slightly distracted by all of the ruckus coming from the front area. He got up to see what was transpiring, and what he saw put a smirk on his face. He stood back, allowing the newcomer to make his debut, greeting the people he knew. Once all the dapping and hugging was over, Major followed him to his room. As he laid the mattress on his bunk, sat down and finally looked up, Major was standing at the foot of his bunk.

He was a little shook at first until he realized who stood in front of him. "Boy!"

"Goddamn, Fresh the prostitutor!" Major said, calling him by the alias only he used.

Fresh stood up and greeted his dawg with some dap.

"What's up with ya', big bruh?"

"Same shit, different day! This life we livin' got us all meetin' up in prison, but what up wit ya' though?" Major inquired, sarcasm lacing his tone.

"Got fucked up, spazzing out on Quies," Fresh said.

"Yeah, yeah. I hear you, but what's really happenin' with ya'? I ain't been hearin' from you like a true dawg shoulda."

"Man, you know how them streets is. Have a nigga head fucked up, but you know how we go," Fresh replied nervously.

"We good though. That's the past, so everythang good with that paper, right?" Major asked.

"I got your paper already put up, but what them crackers talkin' 'bout, bruh? Because Selah act like she don't know shit, and Von been on some other shit lately."

"I ain't been hearin' shit myself. As far as I know, I'm still facing that needle."

"Damn, bruh! We gotta find a way to get you outta here. Can't see losing you to this shit like that."

Fresh was full of hot air. Major didn't respond, just looked at sandbox homie in disgust.

This was supposed to be his right hand. Major wanted to get on his ass, but he had to maintain his composure. Bigger plans were in store. In a few days, niggas would get the shock of their lives.

"Let's go to the day room, the news bout to come on," Major said, then walked off.

Major sat down just in time. The news was just coming on. Fresh sat beside Major, feeling the uneasiness in Major's body language.

"Ladies and gentlemen, the body count is seeming to increase daily on our streets. Yesterday, around five pm, Vinson Tibbs was gunned down on Prescott Road while walking from the Citgo gas station with a female friend, who told authorities that it was a drive by. The shooters were driving a silver Dodge Intrepid. Coincidently, Tibbs was killed two days before he's scheduled to testify against Narcotics Agent, Brian Steeples.

Mr. Steeples is a suspect. We will be sure to keep you updated on the circumstances surrounding this case. In other news, a home invasion occurred at 1247 Hardscrabble Road. Deon Jones was shot several times in the upper portion of his body but is expected to survive his injuries and is in stable condition. Unfortunately, one of the intruders died from a gunshot wound to the chest and head. The other intruder got away. DNA evidence was collected from the scene but will take several weeks to process to learn the identity of the assailant.

If you have any info, please give Crime Stoppers a call. Your identity will remain anonymous."

"What the fuck?" Major said.

"What's up, bruh?" Fresh asked.

"Nigga, that was Maker who killed that nigga."

"For real, bruh? Because Xavier is Trina's lil' cousin' "Sayso", from the Colonies. That lil' nigga been doin' a lot of robberies lately since Vito robbed him."

148

"What Vito robbin' for? I thought you was lookin' out for him?"

"You know that's my partna, but Trina was stealin' dope from me and givin' it to Sayso to sell, but Vito caught on to it and took our dope back and hit the nigga for all his cash too."

Major listened to Fresh, but he wasn't shocked because he always told him about having money and dope around them females. It was no need to lecture him because he would forever be a flashy type of dude for the bitches. That was minor. Major wanted to know what made that nigga target his sister's crib, and he would soon find out .

"Bruh, I'm bout to get me some rest, but wake me up before you bounce. They should be releasing you soon."

"I'll do that, bruh," Fresh replied. Major had heard enough for one day. He didn't want to hear anything else Fresh had to say, and the evening news wasn't any better. He just wanted to relax his mind, body, and soul because when he got out, he had to see about the nigga Sayso and the agent, Brian Steeples. He had a bad feeling about Brian. The lil' dude Vinson just being gunned down like that had to be either done by Brian or one of his cohorts.

"I'ma have to go extra hard at this nigga," Major surmised about approaching the situation with Brian. It was obvious that he wasn't your ordinary narcotics agent. He was crooked and corrupt. Nothing but chains and caskets lied in his wake. Major would have to roll or get rolled the fuck over.

After a few hours of lying down, Major was awakened by Fresh. "Bruh, I'm bout to blow this spot. I'll be in touch. They just called me ATW."

"All the way! Stay up nigga and keep yo' hands to ya' self. You know SC don't play bout that CDV shit."

"I know, bruh." They dapped while Major remained lying down. He was glad to have Fresh out of his presence. Now, all he had to do was get out of jail and get shit straight.

Who Put This Shit Together I'm the Glue...?

"They say I'm fed bound, call me high risk. I'ma full bloodied goon, lames make me sick. You getting three or fo' birds, where I'm from they call you rich," Taliban rapped along as Plies banged through his four twelve-inch Kenwood speakers. He was in his Candy Apple red SS Camaro with white rally stripes, sitting gorgeous on some 26-inch, red Diablo-Spiders. Two Notch Road was super packed because there was a big football game going down, the Palmetto Classics Benedict College vs. SC State. The sun was shining, and women were out choosing, and all the big money bosses were out lurking .

Taliban crept slowly through the bumper to bumper traffic with his Blood brothers trailing behind him in their rides.

His brother, Wayko, was behind him in his cocaine white 81 Camaro Z28 with two tone factory red decals, 24-inch red Lexani rims, and the red, leather interior (representing his blood gang), with the TV in the steering wheel. Coming behind him, was his partner Lump's red and white candy painted, two door Chevy Impala on 26's.

Taliban looked to his left two cars ahead of him and saw Major's homie, Cedric. He looked in their group to see who he knew. "Ain't this 'bout a bitch! Mufucka done beat the system, again!" Taliban said to himself as he quickly searched for a parking spot.

Laid back smoking on a blunt, leaning against a green '08 Tahoe, he noticed a group of hooked up red and white cars on rims pull up where they were tailgating. He simply put his hand on his hip, feeling for his pistol just in case some problems popped off until he noticed his little brothers and a few of their homies .

Now, he saw it for himself. The flashy cars and expensive jewelry made them look like kingpins. All he could do was nod his head and smile. He wasn't a hater and was amazed at how good they were doing for themselves .

"Nigga, what's up?" Taliban said as he walked up and greeted his big brother.

"Ain't shit, but chilling," Major replied.

Wayko and the rest of the crew gathered around, greeting him with love. Some even went in their pockets and gave him money. He knew right then that his lil' brothers were doing the right thing with the work he left them.

After ten minutes of their cars being parked right there on the corner of Two Notch and Elmwood, females began posting up. His brothers had the city on lock.

Major and Taliban were passing a blunt back and forth, sharing laughs, when an orange with white rally stripes Challenger squatting on 26-inch Corleone rims pulled up blasting Webbie's *Savage Life.*

"Look at this dude, here," Taliban said.

"Who that?" Major asked.

"You 'bout to see."

When Fresh stepped out of his car, he had a fifth of Hennessy in one hand and a big blunt in the other. His Coogi Denim outfit was starched to the max as they neatly relaxed at the tongue of matching Coogi boots. The jewels around his neck, ears, wrists, and fingers leaked and stated "I'm ballin'". His drip had definitely sprang a leak.

Fresh dapped up all the homies as he walked through the crowd. When he got to Wayko, then turned around to dap Taliban, "what the fuck?" he said as he froze when he connected eyes with Major. "Nigga, what's happenin'?"

"Ain't shit, what's up?" Major replied.

"If it ain't Whodini in the flesh," Fresh said.

They chopped it up for a few. Really, while Fresh was talking, Major daydreamed at his surroundings. He was thinking about how he could put an event together like this and capitalize off it. He told himself that there was no need to be mad at his brothers and the homies. They exuded typical dope boy behavior. The make money and floss. He just knew how to fuck with them moving forward.

A nice plan formulated in his mind, and he suddenly began to smile and lighten up, but that smile was quickly replaced with a snarl when his eyes fell on the nigga he'd been hoping to see.

Cedric was doing his thing with his partners he worked with, but he glanced at Major every now and then to make sure he was alright. This time he noticed Major was mugging. He followed his eyes quickly, excusing himself from his boys.

Major realized that it was him and damn near blew his top. A dark chocolate, dime piece was sitting shotgun in one of the nicest rides out there. He had to overdo it and out shine the competition: candy green 2010 Camaro SS, sitting on 30-inch green and Chrome Flip Face Corleone wheels, coming through the parking lot, slowly, blasting *Sicko Mode* by Travis Scott.

Major didn't want to start no shit. He came to enjoy himself with his best friend Cedric, who worked an honest job and wasn't with the nonsense anymore, but Major couldn't maintain his composure. No tape was holding his nuts up. Therefore, he had to show niggas that, though he was humble, he was far from pussy.

"Yo' bruh, I see the look in yo' eyes," Cedric said. "Don't do nothin' stupid. You just was let loose. Enjoy ya' freedom."

"Oh, I am," Major lied.

"I just wanna holla at 'em."

Mook didn't see Major posted in the crowd lurking when he parked and eased out of the suicide doors, playing the Big Willie role. The female finally stepped from the vehicle, and, to his surprise, it was Selah, looking classy in a House of Tinks print dress with Giuseppe Zanotti suede pumps. It was too late to turn back because he was already on his way before she stepped from the car. Major didn't care who Selah fucked with. It truly wasn't about her, at all. This was grown man business. He was a boss, a gangster. He had to show who he was and what pedigree he was bred from. Mook owed him money and dodged him for over six months, and now, it was time to pay. By the time Major got to Mook's car, he had come up with the perfect payment.

Mook was being entertained by a few of his boys, so he wasn't aware of his surroundings. Big Ram tried warning Mook about Major, but it was no need. Major was right up on them.

Major spoke to everybody standing around, even Selah. Then he walked up to Mook, headbutted him, and quickly followed with a punch, squaring him in his face. Mook fell to the ground, holding a bloody and broken nose. Major stood over Mook and asked a few questions. "You thought you wasn't ever gon' see a nigga like me again, huh, Mook? You got my mufuckin' money? Huh, nigga? I asked you a fuckin' question?"

"Yeah, Major, man. I got yo' bread, bruh! I got half of it with me right now," Mook said as he looked around hoping one of his boys would help him, but they knew better.

"Babe, I mean, Selah, hand him that bag out the car."

Selah tossed Major the bag of money. He didn't even count it. He just threw it to Wayko who was standing right beside him, Mac 11 in his hands.

"Now, nigga, get the fuck out my way. I'm the glue that put this shit together, and you can't throw me my bread?" Major said, stepping over him and into the driver's side of Mook's car.

"But'cha buying cars, rims, and shit. When you pay the other hunnid grand, you can get'cha whip back," he said as he let down the suicide doors and peeled off, skeeting dirt on Mook and Selah's expensive outfits .

"Man, shit!" Mook said as he got up from the ground.

"Big Ram, take me home."

Wayko looked at Selah and Mook, laughed in their faces, and walked off with the rest of his squad.

Later that night, Major and his squad were at Splurg vibing, having drinks, and catching up on news in the streets. Everyone was partying and enjoying the attention that came along with hood fame. Major was just taking in the progress and popularity of his investment. He had to admit, Majesty and Cedric did one helluva job with the set up and decorations.

There were three bars, all had beautiful Chandelier lights above them. The largest bar was in the center of the club, against a mirrored wall with twelve of the prettiest bartenders you ever seen. The picture booth was to its left, with four pool tables to its right. Across from the photo booth and up six steps was the V.I.P area, with a heart shaped bar with eight bartenders to serve you all the expensive, top notch wine and liquor you desired, complemented by an eight person sized Jacuzzi for reserved members only, just for that night.

Then, you had another bar behind the stage area for the celebrities and other performers of that night.

The club was big enough for them to even fit a boxing ring on the right side of the stage for fight nights. Major was impressed.

"Bruh, what you think about the club?" Fresh asked.

"It's nice," Major replied.

"Ya' boy Cedric been working here since it opened. He act like he owns the place. Whoever the owner is, they let Cedric do things his way. I was thinking about asking him how much the owner would charge me to throw my B-Day party here."

Major took a strong pull from his blunt of Irene and blew smoke in Fresh's face, "holla at him. Since you family, Cedric might put in a good word for you," Major answered nonchalantly, sipping on his drink while coming up with another business idea for the club.

"Alright, bruh. I'm bout to get up on some of these hoes. If you need me, I'll be close by," Fresh said as he blended into the crowd.

Major disappeared into the office area where Cedric was sitting behind a desk counting money, and often glancing at the surveillance cameras.

Without looking up, he knew it was Major who sat on the plush, Gamecock, burgundy crush velvet, Big Easy chair, which comfortably rested against the wall next to the desk because Major was the only other person with the combination to the office's digitally coded pad lock.

"Cedric, what the fuck is that?" Major asked as he noticed Cedric typing on a small machine.

"This is the new 11.6 laptop Lenovo Idea Pad UI Hybrid Notebook that I use to store the money count and keep inventory on the business finances."

"Damn! I need to get one of those for my real estate money I'm 'bout to make."

"I'll get you one tomorrow but get up and let me show you some'n real quick."

Major got up and walked behind Cedric, where he remained seated. Cedric slid his desk chair back a little. He typed a code in the laptop, but before he tapped the last key, "you see this spot right here where my right foot is?"

Major glanced down.

"Watch what happens when I tap this last key on the laptop." He made sure Major was paying close attention while he demonstrated his brilliance.

Cedric tapped the keypad, and Major noticed how the floor quietly opened. The space was the size of a suit case. Cedric took the money he had just counted and placed it in a bookbag. Then, he dropped it inside the hole.

"Now, watch this," Cedric tapped two keys on the laptop, and the floor quietly closed and blended back with the carpet. All of this transpired without a person standing on the opposite side of the desk noticing. The entire operation was fool proof and undetectable.

"That shit crazy, but where does the money go?" Major asked curiously.

Cedric got up and went to the surveillance monitor and showed Major what he came up with. "You see how the trunk of that ugly, rusty-ragged, beat up looking Chevy just opened, shut, and pulled off?"

"Yeah, I see it."

"Well, I had specially built a small tunnel from the floor to the side of the Love Nest where a part of the wall opens, which triggers the trunk to automatically open. Then, while you only see me tapping keys on the laptop, it is alerting Majesty to ease to the car and pull off. That way, no one can rob us. The bag is always secured. Ya' feel me?"

"Damn!"

"Don't worry, I will show you everything you need to know once you're ready because I know you don't want anyone knowing you're the owner. They don't even know Majesty is also a part of the business. She is never here. She just knows what time to pick up and roll out without being seen. But, just to let you know, we've made well over a million already, so bruh, you can leave the streets when you're ready."

"I hear you, but we'll speak on that in 'bout another year or so."

Major looked at Cedric and smiled. "Maybe never!" he said, then walked out of the office.

Pyscho Ass...

Major received word from a few of his partners that some old school cat named Gator had come through their hoods in a green Ford Crown Victoria on rims and robbed them. He knew right then that he had to holler at his daddy before one of them young boys knocked his top off. Major rode through the hood and scooped him up to spend a little time and have a conversation with his old man.

"Pop, I heard you been layin' niggas down! What's up with that?"

"When the old man need a fix and ya' boys on that bullshit, I gotta get mine how the game go," Gator replied.

"What you mean? Them niggas know to look out when you come through."

"Ya' boy Von been playin' fair, but when he was outta town, Fresh wouldn't look out. I started to rob his ass, but instead, I just hit a few hoods that yo' workers didn't hang in."

"Pop, you know if I ain't servin' them, Wayko, Taliban or their boys are."

"I hear you, but you know how it is when you tired of waitin' on the next man. Shid, when that narcotic get ta callin' my name, I gotta answer. If not, I be sick as a damn dog. Those withdrawals kick in fast."

"You mean to tell me, you been hittin' all them niggas by yo 'self?" Major queried incredulously.

"Nah, nigga! 2-Blade rolled wit me, and we handled our business. Them young niggas know the deal," Gator bragged.

"Where my nigga, 2-Blade, at anyway?"

"He probably at home. Let's roll by his crib right quick and holla at him because I ain't see him in a few days."

Major headed to the Colony Projects to holler at 2 Blade, but as they were about to pull into his parking lot, they noticed the dude Blade was talking to wore a police badge on his belt.

"What the fuck?" Major said.

Gator didn't want to accuse his partner of being a snitch, so he just kept quiet and observed the situation as Major turned into the parking lot across from Blade's. Major backed in an empty parking space positioned so they could watch from a distance. The two men seemed very familiar with one another by the way they laughed and joked around. Major saw the two dap and hug, then the officer got in a black BMW truck and drove off.

"Man, we 'll fuck with Blade some other day," Major said as he rode two cars behind the BMW, trying to see the tag number, but the light caught him, and the truck disappeared.

*****

"What the fuck you and the po-po had so much to laugh and joke about out there?" Feebi asked, not liking the scenery she just saw at all.

"Girl, mind ya' damn business," Blade said as he took three porkchops from the refrigerator.

"Mufucka, don't forget, we live in the projects, and if one of these Bloods or Crips start thinkin' we the fuckin' po-po, ain't no way they gon' sell us nothin' or allow us to live out here. That's if they don't kill our asses."

"I ain't sweatin' these lil' niggas out here. Me and Gator will lay all they asses down if we have to. And besides, we ain't gotta buy shit from these lil' niggas. My boy, Vito, is in the area if I need him. He runs shit on this side of town."

"Well, since ya' boy Vito in the area, how 'bout you call and tell him to bring us some'n?" Feebi said ready to abuse Blade's juice card.

"I'm 'bout to eat and play with my daughter. We'll get some'n in our lungs later."

Their daughter Ivory got up from the tv, moving around like she had to use the restroom. Feebi noticed and gave her a *I'ma tear yo' ass up if you piss in them panties* look. Ivory was more than familiar with that look, so she decided to sit down on her Paw Patrol Potty. She was being trained how to go to the restroom on her own, and every now and then, she would piss her panties, but she was tired of the whippings her mother would dish out.

"That's a big girl," Blade said, happy to see his two year old daughter doing good without diapers.

"Nigga, ever since we moved in this damn apartment, you been acting like a bitch gotta beg you to get her high. You already know I'll go and come up with mine though, but I'll be damned if

I'ma go trickin' when you got a pocket full of money and probably dope too."

Section 8 finally came through for Feebi with an apartment. It wasn't a mansion, but she managed with what she had. She ain't have to kiss her mother's ass to sleep on her couch no more or suck Calvin's dirty, small dick to sleep on his stinking ass floor. The two bedroom was spotlessly cleaned, and it looked good for what their limited means could afford.

With Blade's help, they had nice furniture, food, and televisions in each room for their daughter to watch all the cartoons she wanted. Blade received a monthly disability check of $1200. When he had money, Feebi loved him, but when it ran out, she acted as if she couldn't stand his guts. The sight of him alone caused her ass to ache with regret.
When funds were low, he pulled robberies with Gator for extra cash because he loved the thrill of it.

"Blade, call and get us a lil' some'n," Feebi asked politely, now trying to kiss a lil' ass to get high. But she was right when she said Blade probably had a pocket full. He had a few ounces of crack in the house from the robberies him and Gator hit last week, but he was trying to eat and spend a lil' time with their daughter first.

"Woman, I done told you to wait 'til later, and I got you. How the fuck we 'posed to get high with Ivory wide awake anyway?"

Feebi was tired of playing games with Blade. She wanted some crack in her system, and she wanted it right now. Feebi got up from the living room couch, grabbed Ivory's piss pot, and stormed into the kitchen without saying another word.

She poured Ivory's piss in the pan that Blade was frying the porkchops in for her, Ivory, and himself.

"Mufucka! If I can't smoke, y'all won't eat! I don't give a fuck." She stated clapping after each word for emphasis.

"Bitch! What the fuck wrong with you?" Blade said after smacking the fire out of her. He was sick of her ratchet ass.

The slap did nothing to stop her tirade though. "That shit don't hurt. Nigga, I'm a street bitch. I eat them punk ass licks for breakfast," she huffed, stomping off to the kitchen

Ivory started crying. Blade went to comfort his daughter and Feebi went to the refrigerator and started throwing all the food out the door. "You takin' food outta my baby mouth, you junkie bitch! I'm sicka yo' po' ass!" Blade yelled before backhanding Feebi. The blow sent her frail, fragile ass flying across the room.

Blade didn't feel like going through her bullshit. He had too much crack and guns in the apartment. If the police came, their asses were going to jail.

"Nigga, I done tol' you bout yo' goddamn hands!" *Crack!* Feebi shattered a vase over Blade's head. Blood quickly dripped from his wound, snaking down the back of his shirt.

"Daddy!" Ivory hollered now in hysterics. The blow was staggering, causing Blade to lose his footing. He fell back onto the sofa, cupping his head in his hand. Blade winced in pain at the tenderness on the back of his noggin. He pulled his hand back, and his palm was covered in blood.

"Bitch, you draw blood from me as much as I do fa' yo' ungrateful ass?" Blade propelled forward, bouncing off the sofa as if his shoes had springs on the bottom of them. He grabbed her, locked the apartment doors, dragged her in the other room, and beat her crazy ass before fucking her to sleep.

By the time he opened the door to check on Ivory, she had cried herself to sleep outside the bedroom door. Blade knew he had to do something about Feebi's psycho ass. Her drug use was getting out of hand. He wanted to leave her druggie ass, but his love for her wouldn't allow him to walk away. Plus, Ivory needed him. Yet, in his mind, he knew he had to make a change or end up dead or in prison behind Feebi's stupidity.

Gator...

Major went to pick his father up from the hood to take a look at some of the property he bought. He could use his expertise, being that Gator was a certified electrician, plumber, and a well experienced construction worker. As they pulled off from the hood, Major thought about having his dad hire a crew to start fixing on the new properties he would be purchasing in the near future. Then, he remembered that Blade told him he had experience in home improvement, construction, painting, and some more skills that related to fixing on houses.

"Pops, let's get with Blade and see if he wanna get down with us fixin' up these houses I'm 'bout to be buyin'. There's money to be made if y'all with it."

"We can do that because Blade know more about houses than I do," Gator replied. "But what about the shit we saw the other day?"

"I ain't worried 'bout Blade snitchin' on me because if he wanted me knocked off, he coulda been did it. I'll eventually holla at him bout what we saw, but right now, we on some legit shit, so we straight."

"Alright, let's roll," Gator said, happy to hear that Major trusted his partner because he knew in his heart that Blade wasn't a snitch.

As Major got on North Main Street, he thought about how skilled his dad and Blade were and couldn't help but wonder how they got hooked on crack and decided to ask the question he was always so curious about.

"Pops?"

"What's up, son?"

"How you got turned out on that dope?"

Gator looked at Major, wondering why all of a sudden, he asked that question, but he never held nothing back from his kids, and wasn't about to start now.

"A female turned me out!"

Major gave him a crazy look, and Gator was well familiar with the look.

"Yeah, a fuckin' bitch! One day we were at her crib snortin' some coke, and out of the blue, she said that she was tired of hidin' what she did from me. The bitch took some of my cocaine and cooked the shit up and hit it off a soda can and tried passing the shit to me. I slapped the bitch so hard, I knocked her and the crack clear across the room. The bitch told me I wasn't getting no pussy until I at least tried the shit. I wanted some of that bitch some'n bad, so I tried the shit and loved it, and been hooked ever since. I didn't think that anything could hook the old Gator, but boy was I wrong. Yeah, I eventually got that pussy, but I fucked up my life. The only time I was able to stop was when I went to prison and still, the craving haunted my ass where ever I was. I fuck round' and got yo' mama on it, but she quit a few months later and left my weak ass. We'd get back together, and she'd relapse. But ya' mama was determined to get clean and stay clean. She quit that shit cold turkey. Got tired of the life and the bullshit that came along with it and left my ass for good. But no matter what I did, I took care of my kids. Even if I had to rob every dope boy in the city, y'all never went without, and I made sure that all y'all know who the fuck I am."

"Well, all that shit was the past, pops. You done been in them streets gettin' high for too long, and it's time you made a change and enjoy the good life. I'm on like popcorn, daddy, and I need you with me."

"I ain't gon' make no promises, but I'll try, son. The shit is gettin' old. That shit don't even get you high like it used too," Gator said as he lit his Newport, thinking about how life would be without crack.

"That's all I ask. All I need for you to do, is keep me up on my game in these streets, help me wit these houses, and you won't have to worry bout nothin." Major said as he finally pulled up in front of Blade's apartment.

"I got you."

Major got out of his Charger and went to Blade's door and knocked. Feebi answered in some Daisy Duke shorts and a worn out t-shirt, revealing her hard nipples because she wasn't wearing a bra. It looked like she'd been electrocuted the way her hair stood up on top of her head.

"Hey, Major!" Feebi said, opening the door, giving him a big, slutty hug.

Her ass cheeks were hanging out the bottom of her shorts, and her pussy print was bulging so badly, you could see how fat the lips were on her stank looking pussy.

"What's up, Feebi? Where Blade at?"

"Blade at work, why? What he done did now?" she asked thinking it had something to do with that police dude Blade be talking to.

"It's bout some business I need him and my daddy to help me with." Major said, pointing to his car so she could see Gator in the passenger seat.

"Oh, ok! Blade working over at the apartments on Green Street."

"Alright, Feebi, thanks," Major said, about to walk off.

"Aye, Major. Why don't you let a bitch earn a few dollas right quick before you go?"

"Feebi, don't even play ya' self like that," Major responded with his lips twisted at the sides. "Well, let me get a few dollas, so I can get me and my baby some'n to eat."

"Where Ivory at? Neva mind, here," Major said as he went in his pocket and gave her a ten dollar bill and left, knowing exactly what she was up to.

When Major pulled up to Blade's work sight, Blade was just finishing for the day. Blade spotted Gator and Major, said his good byes to his co-workers, and walked over to Major's car.

"What y'all niggas doin' on this side?" Blade asked as he got in the back seat.

"Nigga, I got a business proposition for you," Major said, backing out of the apartments .

"What's that?"

"I want you and Gator to hire a crew of reliable dudes to help fix up the houses and other properties I got and about to buy and guide them to success."

"Shid, when do I start?" Blade said.

"We bout to ride by a few of them now so y'all can let me know what kind of work needs to be done before we put them on the market for sale. I might rent a few out too."

As they headed towards Farrow Road, all Major could think about was the identity of the officer Blade was talking to that day. He was about to ask Blade when his phone rang.

"Excuse me, y'all. Hello?" Major said. "Alright, alright I'm on my way, bye."

"What's going on, son?"

He hung up the phone. "Well, I gotta stop by Alcorn and get Petty right quick. Sonya say the boy was caught smokin' weed in school and the principal wants to lock him up, but that don't sound like nothin' he would do. Petty know better than that shit."

"What?" Gator said, laughing." That lil' nigga act just like you.

"Shid, I wasn't that goddamn bad!" Major said.

"Nah, you wasn't. Yo' ass was worse," Gator said.

Major and Gator tripped a little bit about some of the things Major got into growing up, and Major had to admit that he was a hard headed little dude.

They finally pulled up at Alcorn Middle on Fairfield Road, and Major, Gator, and Blade walked into the school. Major already knew where the principal's office was because he attended the same school growing up. When they stepped inside the office, they were greeted by an elderly black woman who favored Angela Bassett.

"Hello, how may I help you gentlemen?" she asked.

"Hello, I'm Andre Major, this is my father and uncle. I'm here about Petty Major. I'm his uncle."

"Oh, ok. Well, one of our staff walked in the restroom and smelled marijuana. Mr. Major and two of his friends were the only ones in there, " she said, pointing to two other kids whom Major recognized from the hood.

"I had them searched and found over $500 in Petty's pocket. Petty claimed they weren't smoking and that they had just walked in, but where'd he get all that money from is what I want to know."

"Where did he say he got it from?" Major asked her. "He claims he saved it whenever he got money from his mother, father, and uncles."

"Well, that's where he got it from then. As one of his uncles, I own businesses and can confirm that he helps us out when he's not in school, so he should have well over $500." Major said, giving the principal a look of wealth, shattering the stereotype she attempted to place on his nephew.

"We can't do anything to him because he wasn't caught with marijuana in his possession, but please warn him that it's not safe to have that kind of money on him."

"The only reason I got it with me is because I'm going to buy a PlayStation after school," Petty said, lying, and Major knew it. He probably was showing off for some lil' bitty bitches.

"Yes, ma'am. You have a blessed day, " Major said as he began to leave with Petty and his friends in tow.

"Sir, I tried to reached the other two kids' parents, but I wasn't successful."

"Don't worry, I know them and their parents. I'll make sure they get home safely."

*****

After Major dropped off Petty's friends back in the hood, he was back on his mission. He didn't bother to lecture his nephew because he already knew his nephew's involvements in the streets. He'd become a product of his environment. It was just the way he grew up, so fuck it. Petty would roll with them.

Major pulled up to the Casket Gallery and Funeral Home he recently bought on Farrow Road. They looked around. "Shid, son, I think you ought to keep this spot for personal use."

"And do what with it Pops? I don't know shit bout running a funeral parlor."
Gator and Blade exchanged looks. "Nephew think outside the box," he responded, giving him the eye.

"Yep, pull up this stale ass carpet and replace the paint, this spot will come in handy."

As they were leaving, Blade said, "all he need to do now is invest in some hearses." Right then, Major thought about some crazy shit.

"I just might have my old Magnum customized as a casket to sponsor my new business. Think I'll call it Gator-Blade Casket Gallery & Funeral Home. I might just keep the home to cremate some of the bodies I'm bout to catch."

"Now, you thinking like a G. That's what I'm talm 'bout neph. No body, no case. You won't eva' have to worry 'bout shit," Blade added.

"I'm just bullshittin'," Major said, forgetting that Petty's ass knew too much devilment already, but he was serious as a heart attack.

Major finally pulled up on Fontaine Road in front of a big building he'd purchased upon his release from jail. He exited his car and took down the For Sale sign.

An elderly couple with salt and pepper hair pulled in behind them, driving a brand new Mercedes GLE450. Before they stepped outside the vehicle, he overheard Petty say, "See, unc, those the only classes I'm trying to attend."

"Excuse me, sir. Is this place for sale?" the elderly white woman in her mid-sixties asked.

"If you're willing to pay $150,000, it's yours," Major said.

"We'll write you a check for $125,000," the man with her firmly stated.

"That sounds like a deal," Major told him.

"Alright, can we shake on it?" the guy asked, extending his hand to Major .

They shook hands and exchanged cards and decided to close on the deal the following week. Major was a happy man as he headed back to his car with the family behind him.

"Well, ain't no need in viewing this property anymore. I only paid sixty grand for the building," he said, happy to see that this business is easier than he thought.

Major had made a few minor sales previously, but not too big. He made ten grand here, five grand there, but to make over fifty grand, legally, he was in love. He was taken out of his thoughts when his sister called his phone, telling him she was at home and to bring Petty there.

On the way there, Blade started telling him about auctions and other ways to buy property at unbelievable prices. "All that sounds good, Blade. We can jump on that next week."

"Fo'sho."

Major dropped Blade off at his apartment in the Colony and headed to his sister's house.

It Ain't Nuttin' to Cut That Bitch Off...

Major, Gator, and Petty walked into the house where Maker and Sonya were laid back on their sofa with his head laid in her lap. She had tweezers in hand, plucking in-grown hairs from his face.

"Look at this nigga here! What the fuck you getting', a fuckin' facial? Nigga get yo' heavy headed ass off my sister's lap before you crush her thigh bones!" Major said, joking with Maker as he grabbed his ankles slightly pulling him.

Maker quickly hopped up and grabbed Major in a playful tussle. "Nigga, you can't handle me!"

Gator pulled out his .380 pistol from his back pocket and pointed it in their direction. "Sonya, which one do you suggest I shoot?"

"Don't worry, if they break my glass table, I'ma be doin' the shootin'," she replied as she revealed the pink handled, chrome .25 from under her lap .

"None of y'all ain't gon' shoot nothin', so put them popguns back where they came from," Petty said.

"Boy, you better sit on yo' grown ass! That's yo' damn problem now! Don't think I ain't gon' fuck you up for havin' yo' principal call my damn job today. You up there doin' what the fuck you wanna do in those people school," Sonya said.

"Man, that old lady crazy! I may act up, but I ain't crazy enough to smoke no weed in school. I love school cuz that's where all the girls at," Petty said.

"I know that's right!" Maker said.

"Since all my favorite men around, I know I can get me a nice fish aquarium from the Flea Market for real now," Sonya said.

"Let's do it! I need to look around for a few things myself," Major said.

They all loaded up in Sonya's Denali and rode out to the 378 Flea Market. When they arrived, they walked around for about two hours before Sonya found the aquarium she wanted. They were about to leave until he noticed a Mexican staring at him from the jalapeño pepper stand.

"Major! That you, man?" he said.

Major walked a little closer, then he noticed it was Miguel's cousin, Felipe.

"What's happenin', Felipe?" he said.

Felipe came from behind the stand and greeted Major with a firm handshake and a hug. "My friend, where have you been? We miss you, man."

"I been around. What's up, though?" Major asked, getting straight to business.

"Give me yo' number, and you should get a call real soon," Felipe said as he took the card from Major.

"Real Estate, aye? You a smart man, Major. I might have some business for you, but look man, I'll make sho' this number gets in the right hands, ok, my friend?"

"Do that!" Major threw over his shoulder as he walked off.

Less than an hour later, Major was on the phone with the man with the plan, Miguel. They met up the same day and were back to business as usual, but Major still held his grudge for Miguel's abandonment.

*****

Life was treating Major like a true boss. Everything was back on track with Miguel, and Gator-Blade Realty was booming. Today was the day he, Gator, and Blade were to stop by open house in the Winslow community on Sparkleberry Lane.

Business was expanding, and now Major was in full throttle. Everyone introduced themselves, but the host said they were expecting one more guest. Ten minutes later, the front door opened, and Major couldn't believe who the last guest was.

She greeted everyone, but when she got to Blade, she froze for a second before shaking his hand, still in a slight daze,

"You look very familiar! Have we met somewhere before?" she asked.

"No ma'am, I don't think so, but I must say that you are a beautiful sight for any man's eyes," Blade replied.

Finally letting his hand go, "I apologize if I'm wrong, and thanks for the compliment," she said as she turned to greet the next person, but when she turned to face him, she was at a loss for words.

Fresh to death in his maroon Sergio Rossi suit, grey matching blazer, with matching Alejandro Inglemo Gators, Major and Kimiko connected their hazel pupils. Hers instantly watered from the guilt and loving memories of their perfect, passionate past. She was about to greet him with a hand shake like she respectfully did the other real estate agents, owners, and investors, but before she could think of what to do, she was trapped in Major's web. She was still stuck on him emotionally, even though she had did him wrong. She threw her arms around his neck and laid her beautiful, non-made up face on his slender chest, catching a whiff of the smooth, expensive scent of his Creed cologne.

"Baby, what are you doin' here? When did you come home? And, why haven't you called me?" she asked all in one breath.

Politely grabbing her shoulders distancing them slightly, he looked in her eyes. Major licked his pink, full-lips, then brushed his thumb and index fingers smoothly across his perfectly trimmed mustache.

"I'm here on business as a realtor. I came home months ago, and I didn't call you because I'm focusing on me and the things I have to do to keep myself happy and successful." He let go of her shoulders with his other hand. Kimiko wasn't prepared to see him again. She couldn't believe that he was actually home, dressed the way she always pictured, and making a career within real estate, without her assistance. Something she basically forced in his lap. She knew that he had to be doing very well to be in the company of her father and his business associates.

Everyone was curious as to how Kimiko and Mr. Major knew one another. Gator and Blade weren't too shocked though, because they knew he was the man.

"Well, ladies and gentlemen! Now that we are all here and well acquainted, I guess we can begin with business," Mr. Perez stated.

Mr. Perez was hosting open house and Major had met him at a few auctions. Mr. Perez was also Kimiko's father. He had no idea that the guy under his tutelage was a kingpin, whom his daughter was madly in love with.

The meeting was inspirational and motivating. When it was over, Major said his goodbyes and headed to his brand new White Audi Q5. As he, Gator, and Blade were closing their doors, Kimiko stopped him.

"Major, let me speak with you for a sec." Kimiko said, as she basically ran to his car.

"Yeah, what's up?" he answered with sarcasm in his tone.

"When can I spend some time with you?"

"For what? You left ya' boy hangin' when ya' thought I wasn't ever goin' to see the streets again, so why I should waste my time now with yo' disloyal ass?"

"Because I love you! I miss you! And, I'm sorry for not coming to visit you, but I never experienced nothing like that! Just give me another chance."

"Don't be sorry, be mindful. No excuses! You did what was best for you, now move around. I have to go. If it's meant to be, it'll happen," Major said. Then, he closed his door and backed out of the parking lot, leaving her standing there looking stupid.

Kimiko walked to her car looking like she lost her best friend. She didn't see her father standing in the door way watching as she backed out and drove home thinking of a way to find Major and get back in his good graces.

On the way back to their world, Gator and Blade asked Major a million and one questions. "Son, that's a bad bitch. Mixed breed, cat eyes, smart. Lawd, have mercy."

"Sho' is, where you meet her at?" Blade quizzed.

Major let out an exasperated sigh, "I've been knowing her for a while, three years to be exact. Wanted to marry her ass, but she turned her back on me. These hoes ain't loyal."

"Nigga, I know you a boss and all, but I taught you better than to throw away yo' meal ticket. Nigga, you gotta keep yo' enemies close and utilize them and their resources to the fullest," Gator said.

"Yeah, pop, I guess you right, but she turned her back on me. A nigga came outta that shit and bounced back, handsome and wealthy. I'll fuck with her when I'm ready," Major said as he thought about everything Gator was telling him. He had to put his pride to the side and figure out a way to utilize Kimiko and benefit from the access she had in the real estate world and so much more.

*****

Major and Fresh sat in the STS Cadillac in the parking lot of Sonya's new business. She named it Petty Change Dry Cleaners on North Main Street. Major got her started because his big sister has had his back since he got started in the dope game. Actually, she gave him his second package, and as he got older, she would give him money to flip from her income tax checks. Sonya had been doing dry cleaning for over ten years. Sick of seeing those closest to him slaving while working hard for others, Major felt it was time to make her an owner. He caught a sweet deal on the building when the previous owners felt they were too old to stay in business. They lost interest, had no kids or grandkids who would keep it going, so they decided to sell.

Major had picked his niece, Crystal, up from school and was dropping her off to help her mom, which was her job every day after school. Before they pulled off, Major was on his UI Hybrid laptop his homie Cedric bought him showing Fresh what he was having done to his Magnum. He was getting ready to kill the competition at the car shows this summer.

"Boy, you actin' ignorant!" Fresh said.

"You ain't seen shit. Wail til' it's done, " Major bragged.

"Excuse me, bruh. Hello?" he said, answering his phone.

Major hit the horn, letting his sister know he was leaving.

He backed out of the parking lot once she waved goodbye to him. He headed to his spot in Northwood Hills to grab the work his associate had just ordered.

"Bruh, we gotta make a move in Tiffany Gardens right quick. You got time to roll wit me up there?" Major asked.

"Let's do it! I ain't got shit goin' on right now".

Major pulled up to the house where he had the work stashed.

"Who shit this is, bruh? It's nice," Fresh asked.

"This one of the houses I got for sale. I'm just using it until I get a buyer," Major answered as he got out of the car. He opened the door with his key, walked straight to the back door, and hopped the fence to the house next door where the product was actually being held.

Fresh was his partner, but Major trusted no one, especially after everyone showed their true colors when he was locked up. He led Fresh to believe that he trusted him, but Fresh nor anyone else would ever know exactly where he kept his stashes and how he operated. He grabbed the half of brick for his client and two more for Fresh, then he hopped the gate, walked back through the back door and out the front door, just like Fresh had seen him do. When he got in the car, he handed Fresh the bag containing the two birds.

"We gon' drop yo' shit off at one of yo' spots, then we'll go see my peoples, alright?" Major said.

"That's what it is! Take me by Quies since it's on the way."

Major shook his head and headed to Lincolnshire. He didn't understand Fresh. He put too much trust in females. They arrived at Quies's, and Major's cell went off with a number he wasn't familiar with. He thought about ignoring it but decided to answer anyway.

"Aye, Major. I'll be right back," Fresh hopped of out the car and ran inside the house. When he came back, Major was looking upset. "Why you lookin' crazy all of a sudden?"

"Because, I just got a call from Wayko. He's in jail. I need to go see what's up with him."

"Nigga, handle yo' business! I'll go see yo' people for you."

"That's what it is," Major said as he dapped Fresh up.

Fresh exited the car and hopped in his Tahoe. He backed out behind Major and headed to Tiffany Gardens. Major headed to Wayko's mother's house and told her that he needed her to go and pay Wayko's bond. She was on that shit, so Major had to physically take her to the bondsman, or she'd put his money in the air.

*****

Fresh pulled up to Tuck's trailer. A tall, muscular, dark skinned dude walked from behind Tuck's trailer and to Fresh's passenger door. Fresh grabbed his pistol, pointing it at dude's noggin. The man threw his hands in the air.

"Hold, Hold! Man, I'm Tuck people. He called you for me! "

Fresh cracked his window slightly, "nigga, hold up! Where the fuck Tuck at?"

"He ain't here, but I got all the money right here," he said, revealing the stacks of money in a tote bag that was slung over his shoulder. Fresh let his guard down once he saw green presidents and unlocked his door.

"You got the half of chicken like I ordered?"

"Yeah, I got it, but who the fuck you is, my nigga?" Fresh asked.

"They call me Pressure, bruh," he said, extending his hand, but Fresh left it hanging.

Fresh reached under his seat. By the time he came up with the work, Pressure already had his .38 snub nose pointed at him.

Fresh saw the gun and dropped the half a brick in his lap from shock. He couldn't believe he fell for the okey doke.

"Nigga, hand me that fuckin' work before I knock the meat out yo' taco," Pressure warned, chambering a round as he leaned his right shoulder to the passenger side window while keeping his pistol pointed at Fresh's face. Fresh felt sick and couldn't believe that he allowed himself to get caught up in such a way.

"Bruh, you ain't gotta point that shit in my fuckin' face. If you gon' rob me, just get this shit and let me get the fuck on, but if you gon' shoot," Fresh said, then he frisbeed the half a brick in Pressure's face, hitting him across the bridge of his nose. Fresh tried grabbing the gun, but being quick to squeeze, Pressure applied pressure to the trigger. *Pop! Pop!* Hot bullets tore through his flesh as he cried out in pain. "Uhhhggh! Shit!" Fresh moaned but kept fighting for his life. Pressure wouldn't let go of the trigger, so Fresh decided to keep enough grip on Pressure's hand and wrist so that he wouldn't hit the lower part of his body.

As planned, Pressure was forced to shoot Fresh in the legs until his revolver ran out of bullets. Now, Pressure fought to get the upper hand on Fresh and find out where he had his pistol. Pressure rapidly and powerfully chopped Fresh across the side of his head and face with his empty pistol, but Fresh kept reaching under his left thigh for his 9mm while trying to ignore the pain in his abdomen. He'd been hit four times out of six rounds.

Fresh's entire body felt hot, as if someone had set his ass on fire. Time seemed to be moving slowly as he fought to survive. Fresh was determined to make it out of this situation with his life. He felt himself growing weak. The gunshots had taken some of the fight out of him. Just when Fresh's body wanted to give in, Pressure grew fatigued. He grabbed the latch to the door, opened it and grabbed the coke, then quickly hopped out of Fresh's truck. Fresh couldn't believe his luck.

God had answered his silent prayer to save him once again.

Fresh grabbed his gun and shot at Pressure a few times. *Boom! Boom! Boom!* Fresh's cannon shot slugs, catching Pressure in the shoulder, partially opening his back up. Bullets dented the trailer, whizzing past his head as he quickly disappeared behind the trailer. Fresh wanted to give chase but was fucked up himself. He needed medical attention and fast. Fresh threw his truck in reverse and backed up hoping to see his target, but all he saw was four more dudes running towards him busting.

Doom! Doom! Doom!

Bop! Bop! Bop!

Pop! Pop! Pop! His windshield shattered before caving in. Shards of glass bit into his head and upper body. A barrage of hollow points pelleted his whip as he peeled out rushing to escape losing his life. In a panic, he dialed Major's phone, constantly checking over his shoulder to make sure he wasn't being followed. "Fuck!" he hollered when Major didn't answer.

Fresh was losing a lot of blood quickly, so on his way to meet Vito, he called an ambulance.

"Excuse me, I've been shot numerous times and I'm losing a lot of blood," Fresh uttered growing winded. Pain coursed throughout his body. Every fiber of his being ached. "I'm at McDonald's on North Main Street. Please, send me some help," he continued before disconnecting the call and calling Vito back.

"Bruh, where you at?"

"Nigga, I'm pullin' up."

"Ok, I 'm bout to be sittin' down inside. Get my pistol out my truck from under the seat because the police and ambulance are on the way. I'll call you from the hospital."

"Say no more, bruh."

Fresh climbed out of the truck, struggling to stand on his feet. The pain that ripped through his legs was indescribable. Blood saturated his denims as he took baby steps to enter the fast food eatery. His head spun on his neck. Everything around him appeared to be moving at an accelerated pace. He staggered. "Come on, Fresh. You almost there," he coached, willing himself to push forward but his will wasn't strong enough. Fresh collapsed in the middle of the parking lot, succumbing to his injuries.

*****

As Major and Wayko sat in Mom's Kitchen conversing over lunch about the situation, Wayko began to piece together what got him in the predicament with the gun.

"So, you got pulled over, and?" Major questioned waiting for his little brother to finish the sentence.

"Yeah, bruh. They told me they had a warrant for me. I thought it was for an old ticket or some'n, but when I got to bond hearing, they started talkin' 'bout I ran from him at Alcorn Middle School. Say, I threw the gun, and a student found it the next day under a teacher's car and reported it to the principal. They called the police, and my fingerprints were found on it. I didn't know what the fuck they were talkin' 'bout 'til they showed the gun in an evidence bag in court."

"Was it one of yo' guns?" Major asked.

"Hell yeah! It was my chrome .380 wit the gold trigger. I gave it to my ol' lady a few months back."

"How the hell it got to the school, though?"

"Nigga, I let Petty spend the weekend with me and the gun came up missin'. Bruh, we gotta do some'n 'bout his lil' wild ass because now, I'm facing some bullshit because of his stupidity, tryna be grown. We gotta keep him away from our lifestyle. His young and dumb ass is being exposed to entirely too much."

"Bruh, you right, but don't sweat that gun charge. It'll get thrown out," Major said as he looked at his phone and realized he had several missed calls. "Damn, fuckin' wit you I forgot my phone was still on silent."

Major viewed his missed call log and realized that Vito, Fresh, Quies, and Mrs. Drake(Fresh's mom) had called him. He called Fresh's mom first. He knew something tragic had to occur if she was calling. *Lord, I hope my boy ain't dead. Please not right now.* He thought fearing the worst.

"Major, Phillip is in the hospital!" she yelled. Major could tell she was crying.

"What happened?"

"He's been shot."

"When this happened?" Major asked.

"Yesterday."

"Damn! I'm on the way," Major hung up. "Come on, Wayko, Fresh in the damn hospital. Major got up and left a ten dollar tip before briskly walking to the door.

"What happened, bruh?" Wayko asked getting up from his seat, following Major out to the door.

"Somebody opened his ass up. We finna find out," he tossed over his shoulder.

No Body, No Case...

Sayso was laying low ever since he'd been robbing all of Vito's workers. Things had been fucked up for him. Every time he turned right, things went left, but he really messed up when he robbed and stabbed Jab and didn't kill him. Now, he had wild ass Dip and the whole Bishop Projects after him. Most of them boys were Crip and Folk, so he had to watch himself in certain areas. Sayso was a Blood from the Colony, but he was a wanted man for robbing within his own crew. He wasn't thinking clearly when things were going down, and, if caught slipping, he was surely a dead man.

One day, he was at Trina's spot when Mook came over. They smoked a few blunts and chopped it up. Mook remembered Trina telling him how her cousin was wild and thugged out, so he decided to use that to his advantage. They started hanging and Mook told Sayso he had a few licks lined up for him, but one being in particular.

"Who you talkin' 'bout, Mook?" Sayso asked.

"The nigga name Major. You ever heard of him?"

"Yeah, but if he got *major* cash, I'm wit it!"

"Alright, I'll get back at you on it in a few days."

Sayso had heard many whispered conversations regarding Major and knew it would be a dangerous mission going after a nigga of his caliber, but money talked, and bullshit could float a million miles. He made a few calls and recruited some thoroughbreds he felt could handle the weight of a caper of this magnitude. He hollered at Trina and asked her what she thought about it.

"Boy is you crazy? You need to stay outta that one and let Mook handle his own beef with Major. He's a dangerous ass nigga, cuz, and if you heard anything about that nigga, believe all that shit! I know you can hold yo' own in them streets, but Major is my friend, Fresh's partna, and they don't do nothin' but murk niggas. Besides, he a good dude who will put you on if I holla'd at him for you," Trina said.

Sayso grew quiet. Trina could tell that the gears in his mental were grinding. "On some real shit, ain't nobody tryna do fish fries and set up go fund me pages to bury yo' hot ass. Leave that one alone. I'm telling you. Those niggas ain't what you want," she warned.

Sayso heard her out but decided to take his chances.

All he was waiting on was for Mook to give him the word.

Maker received a call from his homie Pressure, telling him about a lick he had lined up with one of his lil' homies and needed him to roll because it was supposed to be a lot of cash involved and maybe some gun-play also.

"Who you talkin' bout, P?" Maker asked.

"Some nigga, name Major. You know' em?"

"Nah, but who the lil' nigga you spoke of that's lining this shit up?" Maker said.

"This lil' nigga, Sayso from the Colony."

"Alright, bruh. I'm in, just keep me up on game."

*****

Monday morning at 6 am sharp, Sayso and the crew he assembled hid in the woods on Sparkleberry Lane. Mook informed Sayso that he followed Major to that house on numerous occasions, and if the White Audi Q5 was there, to execute the plan. That was the house Major had bought from Mr. Perez, Kimiko's father, and started hosting his very own open house to promote and advertise the properties he had for sale.

Major slept there from time to time, but always left for the city between 6:30-7:00 am. Major walked out of his front door and placed the 803 Duffle Bag in his trunk, then walked back inside the house, leaving the front door wide open.

"Alright, y'all, it's now or neva. Let's body this nigga, and take his product," Pressure said to the young soldiers, Maker and Sayso.

They all ran from the woods, which were directly across the street from Major's house. They entered the home and spread out quickly inside the house with guns drawn. In a crouched position, Sayso maneuvered about the home's interior. Sweat beaded his face. His anxiety level was on ten. Something about the entire ordeal felt off. An inner voice screamed for him to turn back. *Fuck that shit. I'm in here now. I ain't leavin' without that paper and product,"* Sayso bent the corner and nearly dropped his weapon at the sight before him. The blood in his face drained into his belly. He felt sick.

Major watched the color flee from Sayso's body. He appeared gray standing before him with that weak ass 9 mm compared to his army edition .50 caliber machine gun pointed in his direction.

"Oh, shit!" Sayso said shocked and scared as hell of the weapon Major possessed.

Major stood from the plush white leather couch he'd been sitting on with his weapon hoisted on his shoulder but trained at Sayso's top piece. A door closed behind them. His cohorts were coming to his aide. A feeling of relief washed over Sayso. His crew was coming to his rescue. "You might as well run that shit. You know what it is, mane." Sayso stated with bravado, poking his chest out a little. He had the drop on Major. Today, a kingpin would be exed out by a block boy. Street fame and respect awaited him.

"I'm in here y'all," he threw over his shoulder, afraid to take his eyes off of Major.

Major stood stoic, a smirk tilting his lips. "Bust ya' gun then, youngin'. I'll die before I let ya' punk ass do me dirty."

Maker had his .223 assault rifle glued to Pressure's temple.

"What the fuck is goin' on, Maker?"

"Nigga, Major is my brother, and we do everythang together, but toe taggin' pussy niggas like you is our specialty."

"Ahhh shit!" Sayso said as he saw Vito come from the back room with a ML 10 Sniper Rifle, 300 rounds, with a clip on nightlight just in case.

"Umm hum, you ain't expect to see me, did you?" Vito said as he held his weapon to Sayso's head. "Yee—Yee," Vito yelled his special code, and in came two more of Major's killers. Sayso's eyes damn near popped out of his head when he saw Dip and Jab come from the kitchen with their .40 Glocks in their hands. Jab walked up to Sayso and bashed him in his face with the butt of his gun. Sayso crumpled to the floor. Jab kneeled beside him and relieved him of his weapon.

"You won't be needing this where you goin', my nigga!"

Dip took Pressure and the other lil' homies' guns, then they heard a knock at the door while binding their hostages. Major already knew who was at the door.

"Come in!" Major yelled.

Pressure couldn't believe his eyes. He was mainly on this lick because he thought he was about to rob Major twice, but when Fresh walked in with a slight limp- he knew his family would need to make funeral arrangements. Pressure assumed that Fresh was Major the other day, but Major couldn't make it, so now his mind was confetti. His thoughts were all over the place.

"What the fuck?" Fresh said as he froze from seeing Pressure's face, "Major, this the nigga who shot me," he said, pulling out his gun.

"Hold up, bruh. Not here. I got some'n else in store for these mufuckas," Major said.

"Alright, I can dig it, but what the fuck kind of guns you and Vito holdin' and where mine?" Fresh said.

"This millionaire shit, my nigga. Don't trip, I got some'n special for you," Major boasted.

"Now, Sayso, who put you on this lick?"

With so many weapons pointed in his face, Sayso realized that the odds were against him. He started spilling his guts. If he was going to die, Mook's ass was riding shotgun with him to hell.

"Nigga named Mook."

"Mook? Where that nigga at?" Dip and Jab both grunted simultaneously.

"That nigga think it's a game. Where can we find that nigga at?" Major asked through clenched teeth. It was time he bodied Mook once and for all. He was tired of playing with that nigga.

"He's at my cousin, Trina's spot, waitin' for my return," Sayso added throwing Trina under the bus with him.

"What damn Trina?" Fresh asked dumbfounded. He didn't want to believe that his bottom bitch was in on setting his team up to take a fall.

Major sucked his teeth answering the question for Sayso, "Nigga, what Trina you think? Tender dick ass nigga."

Vito said, "This the lil' nigga I took yo' dope and money from. I saw her talking to this nigga a few weeks ago in the Colonies. He ain't lying. She in on this shit too. I put money on it."

"Who you?" Sayso asked.

Fresh karate kicked Sayso in the mouth, cracking his jaw. "You don't ask me shit, nigga. With'cho pussy ass. Say your prayers. We burying yo' ass this day."

The crew witnessed the look of embarrassment spread across Fresh's face. While Major's expression said *I told you so* without him even opening his mouth.

Dip spoke up, "Mook been fuckin Trina for months now, and he never could stand Major."

"Oh, yeah? Well, I'll pay him a visit after I deal with y'all slimy ass niggas. Bruh, load these niggas up in the van out back."

They hogtied Sayso, Pressure, and Sayso's little homie, then they covered their heads and stuffed them into the Casket Gallery van. Pressure knew that this shit was really serious now, so he started copping pleas with Maker, but it was too late.

"Please, Maker, man. Don't let' em do this shit to me dawg. We grew up together. Think 'bout my mama man. You know her heart bad. This will take her out."

"Leave Ms.Glodine outta this. She old anyway and you wasn't thinkin' bout'cha mama when you wanted to body my nigga."

For the remainder of the ride, silence filled the van. Only sniffling and heavy breathing could be heard from the rear. One of those niggas had pissed and shit themselves because the van smelled like a dirty baby's diaper. Fifteen minutes later, Major pulled up to his Casket Gallery. He parked in the back of the building and had his squad bring the hostages through the rear of funeral home. When they walked down stairs to the basement, they could feel the heat from the crematory furnace.

"What the fuck is that smell?" Sayso asked, talking while his face was still covered.

"Nigga shut the fuck up. We bout to die and you asking questions," the young nigga with them stated.

"Y'all 'bout to see," Major replied.

Major opened the crematory furnace and looked at his crew. "Have y'all ever deep fried a nigga?"

"Hell nah, nigga!" they answered in unison.

"Well, say hello to the next level of takin' a life! Now pick which one we gon' roast first!"

They were all frozen in shock, thinking Major was bullshitting, until Major grabbed the smaller one and pushed him in the scorching hot furnace kicking and screaming. "Arrrghhhh, Arrrghhhh!" His blood curdling screams caused Sayso to both wet and shit himself.

Snot dripped from his nose, falling into his mouth. With the burlap sack still covering his face, he had no idea what happened. All he felt was hellish heat.

After only a few seconds, his comrade's screams ceased. Dip and Jab snatched the sacks from Pressure and Sayso's faces. "From dust you were formed, to dust you will return." Fresh stated evenly, eulogizing the men that had brought him harm.

"Help him toss they asses in, so we can haul ass. I'm hungry," Maker stated, rubbing his rotund belly.

Dip grabbed Pressure under the shoulders as Jab secured his feet. Pressure bucked like a bull trying to escape his fate. Fresh walked over, striking him in the forehead with the butt of his gun causing Pressure to fold like a deck of cards. The blow knocked him out.

"This nigga is heavy as fuck," Jab complained.

They tossed him into the furnace. As soon as the dancing fire touched his skin, he hollered while thrashing helplessly within the flames.

Sayso shook loose from Fresh's grasp, attempting to make a run for it. "Catch his ass." *Pop! Pop!*

Maker fired two shots, a bullet catching him in each leg. "Nobody ain't 'bout to chase yo' ass." Maker and Major each hoisted Sayso up under his arms, dragging him to his death on his knees. They flung him into the crematory furnace on top of Pressure. The sounds of his screaming and yelling were deafening to anyone's human ears. The burning, popping, and smell of flesh sent chills travelling down their spines and caused goosebumps to blanket their arms.

"From this point forward, this is how we'll dispose of all trash. No body, no case."

Don't Underestimate a Gangsta...

So much had transpired in the past few weeks with Major's business in the streets. Niggas were robbing and shooting his workers, and those closest to him were becoming shiesty. His house in Northwood Hills was broken into. He knew Fresh had something to do with it because he was the only person with knowledge about that spot. Greed disrupted the trust he had in his homie. Tuck was found dead in his trailer after neighbors complained of smelling a foul odor, and now Miguel was hollering about there being a drought on product because one of his boats was raided at the loading dock in Charleston, South Carolina.

Miguel offered Major to take a trip out of town with him to relax their minds until things were straight with the work. Major needed a vacation to clear his mind. He was seriously contemplating having Fresh cremated. This trip with Miguel would act as the perfect distraction to ease his mental.

Miguel owned several acres of land in Dallas, Texas, where he lived on a big farm. He grew vegetables, bred horses and cows, fought chickens, and of course, stashed cocaine and marijuana.

Major enjoyed his time in Texas with Miguel. He met a lot of his family and friends. After spending a few days on the dude's ranch, they flew privately to California.

Miguel also owned land on Pebble Beach. Major smoked on some of the best weed ever in Cali.

Miguel showed Major a good time there also, but it was time they stopped by Las Vegas and do some gambling. When they arrived in Las Vegas, they stayed at the Trump Casino Hotel where they met with Miguel's brother, Juarez, and his two younger cousins, Beecho and Alejandro, who were from Acapulco, Mexico. This was their first time being stateside, and they didn't plan on staying in the US too long. Miguel had them there on official business, but he wanted them to enjoy themselves before they headed back to Texas to deal with the Mendoza Family for robbing his shipments.

After a long weekend in Vegas, they finally arrived back in Texas. Miguel received word that the Mendoza family had fled upon his arrival and were seeking refuge in Hereford, Texas.

Over dinner, Miguel laid down the plan to his cousins of how he wanted them to execute the hit against the Mendoza's during a drug transaction they were scheduled to make. Major sat back and listened, realizing that Miguel was very reckless with the way he handled business. This wasn't Mexico. The crimes they got away with on their soil could get you the needle in the United States. Extreme caution needed to be taken, but this wasn't Major's job and his input wasn't asked so he remained silent.

The very next morning, Miguel and Major sat across the street parked in a black Avalanche in the Family Dollar parking lot, watching the Ace Rental Center van leaving the company's property with a hundred kilos of pure Mexican cocaine. Miguel's cousins were supposed to bum rush them a few blocks up the road, but the Hereford County Police pulled them over for a busted break light. "Dios mio!"

Miguel's cousins fell back, but Miguel wanted them to get that coke by any means necessary.

"What the fuck are they doin?" Miguel shouted, growing angry. He snatched the Stetson from his head and slammed a closed fist against the dashboard. Major continued to trail them a few paces behind.

The two men driving the Ace Rental Center van weren't authorized drivers. Therefore, they were either going to go to jail, take the cops on a high-speed chase, or have a shoot-out.

"You see this shit, Major? Me had them come all the way from Mexico to handle shit like this, but dem made me waste time and money. A hundred fuckin' kilos 'bout to be confiscated," he slammed the dashboard again, having a complete fit in his seat.

"For the money I pay them, those pigs are supposed to be dead."

"Hand me yo' gun, Miguel. We getting' those bricks," Major informed. " 'bout to show you how we do shit where I'm from."

"Major, what the fuck are you talkin' 'bout? You are a hustla, not a robber."

"Miguel, you got me all the way fucked up. I'm a fuckin' gangsta. We hustle, rob, steal, and kill, when necessary. Right now, this shit is necessary. Hand me yo' iron and meet me back at the Family Dollar."

Major hopped out the passenger side of the Avalanche. He took off his jacket, then his t-shirt, using it to cover his face. Then, he put back on his jacket and did what he did best.

As they pulled to the shoulder of the road, he observed the officer's radio in their tag number. Major wasted no time. He crept up on the passenger side of the police cruiser so passing traffic couldn't see him, and once he was directly at the door from a kneeling position, Major unloaded his .40 Cal and shot the officer in his right temple, causing blood to pepper the officer's face in the driver's seat. Brain matter that resembled spaghetti coated the windshield.

The other deputy sat frozen in shock for a brief second. He moved to retrieve his weapon but was too slow. *Boom! Boom!* Hollow points lifted him from the seat before slamming him back down as his chest exploded.

Boom! Boom! Major hit him two more times for good measure. A bullet ripped through his neck. The second shot entered one ear and exited out the other.

Major ran to the Ace Rental Center van, which was only a few feet ahead. He walked to the back of the van, opened it, and got in.

The guys in the van were just some regular guys with no guns . They were scared shitless, not believing what they'd gotten themselves drawn into.

"Ok, you two, I need for y'all to get out and lock yo' selves in the back seat of the police car, or I'm killin' you both."

The two white guys looked at one another and got out of the van, running towards the police car, and did as told. Major mashed the gas, driving off leaving dust and death in his wake. When he got by Family Dollar, he called Miguel.

"Follow me," Major said driving by in the Ace Rental van.

"I don't believe this shit," Miguel mumbled to himself. He was in awe at Major driving the van containing all that product.

He followed Major a few blocks up the street. Major pulled over. Then, they loaded the boxes of cocaine into Miguel's truck and pulled off with Beecho and Alejandro following them. They got back to Miguel's farm where Miguel murdered both of them in front of Major, then fed their bodies to his hogs.

They left out for Carolina. Miguel had his people bring the work behind them. He gave Major half of the coke. From that moment, Miquel developed a new level of respect for Major. The young man seated next to him was a savage in every sense of the word.

*****

Major was leaving from having a friendly dinner with Quies at Olive Garden on Two Notch Road. His balls and word were solid, so, upholding the promise he made to her when she visited him in county was a no brainer. Plus, he wanted to pick her brain regarding Fresh. That nigga was moving foully, but he kept the snake around in hopes of weeding out the rats.

While in route to the city, Major noticed a Suburban SUV and Yukon, both black trailing him. He clutched his .45 and kept riding, but applied pressure on the petal to increase speed. Noticing he was getting further away, his pursuers sped up and opened fire on him from each side of Major's car.

Tat! Tat! Tat! Tat!

Boom! Boom! Boom!

Pop! Pop! Pop! Heavy artillery pelleted his whip, shattering the windows. Shots ripped up the dashboard, headrest, and his CD player. Hot metal tore through his flesh as bullets exploded inside his body. Several bullets riddled his frame.

Major ducked in an attempt to dodge being hit, but his efforts were futile. The gunfire went on without ceasing, tearing his ass up.

Panicked, Major, hit the gas on his STS, making them to give chase. They weren't able to keep up, but they weren't too far behind him either. Through labored breaths, he phoned Wayko. "Bruh, rally the team up and have er'body on standby. I'm being chased and shot at. I've been hit," he gave descriptions of both trucks following him before disconnecting the call. His body was set ablaze with heat as he struggled to keep the car on the road. Adrenaline pulsing through his veins is what propelled him forward. He didn't know who was shooting at him or why, but he was determined to live.

His crew already knew what to do. When Major rode through Gable Oaks Projects, Wayko, Taliban, Lump, and about twenty more Bloods were waiting with all kinds of artillery locked, loaded, and ready to slaughter whoever it was pursuing Major. Just as Major's whip rounded the corner, the back tires were shot out causing him to careen off the road. His whip was smoking from all the hot shots being fired at it. Major was driving so fast that he lost control of the vehicle, and it flipped onto its side. "Goddamn it!" Major groaned as the bullets kept coming. 'These niggas ain't playin!" he hollered, feeling the pain coursing through his body.

The trucks couldn't see what they were driving into, until they pulled completely into the parking lot. Several armed men hopped out of the SUVs donning black clothing with full intentions of finishing Major off. That's when they noticed what looked like a small army of thugs dressed in red, descending upon both vehicles. Guns fired from all directions. As they tried backing up, bullets stormed in on their vehicles from every angle.

It sounded like fireworks being set off at a New Year's celebration as a cacophony of shots rang out. After what seemed to be an eternity, Wayko threw his hand the air, calling for the firing to cease. He motioned for a few soldiers to check out the damage as he jogged towards Major to check on him, his heart hammering in his chest as fear of discovering the worst overtook him.

Wayko tossed his gun onto the pavement as he pulled on the door handle to gain access to Major. There were so many bullets planted into the frame of his whip that the door handle was hot to the touch.

Wayko pulled Major's unresponsive body from the car. Tears fell from his eyes as he saw the lifeless expression on his friend's face. His eyes were still open, body drenched in blood.

There were holes everywhere with blood oozing out of them. "Help!! Help! Somebody call for help!" Wayko yelled.

A few of their soldiers ran over to offer aide to Major, but there was nothing they could do. Major was gone. Wayko swallowed his tears, closing Major's eyes before laying him in the grass on his back.

Wayko retrieved his weapon from the ground and walked over to the Burban where two white men and one black guy were dead inside the vehicle. Wayko walked up and checked their pockets, found nothing, but he noticed one of the white guys was still alive, struggling to breathe. He grabbed the man's gun, putting that steel against his temple. "Who the fuck sent you?"

"Brian. Brian Steeples," he uttered tiredly before taking his last breath."

STAY TUNED...

Connect With Me On Social Media
Instagram: @Blackberry_Poppins
Facebook: Alechy Sumter
Email: alechysumter@gmail.com

Millionaire Dreams

CPSIA information can be obtained
at www.ICGtesting.com
Printed in the USA
LVHW041551060219
606606LV00002B/316/P

9 781729 143100